MEMENTO MORI

Copyright © Lee Stevens 2014

First Published 2014

This Edition Published 2021

For Jack and Amy

"The boundaries which divide Life from Death are at best shadowy and vague. Who shall say where the one ends, and the other begins?"

Edgar Allan Poe

"See my hands and my feet, that it is myself. Touch me, and see. For a spirit does not have flesh and bones as you see that I have."

Luke 24:39

1
BEFORE WE BEGIN...

If, like myself, you have ever been haunted, then you will understand why I feel compelled to recount the following tale. You will also understand why it has taken me almost forty years and until the age of seventy-three to do so. You see, for the longest time I have been unwilling to share my story with others, not out of fear of ridicule, but more that I have always been too uncomfortable to talk about what happened all those years ago. That is until now, as I am old, and I believe that this is a story that should not die along with me. So here I am, writing these words for someone to hopefully read one day and make of it what they will.

I must stress that I experienced everything you are about to read, although to this day I am still unsure about what was real and what was not. However, the people involved are very real (or *were*, I should say, as many of them are long since dead) but out of respect I have changed many of their names. I have also done the same with certain buildings, streets, and other locations to provide even more anonymity to those that were involved, both the innocent and the evil.

All my details, however, are very true.

My Name is Charles Attwood. My father was an Englishman by the name of James Arthur Attwood who was born into comfortable wealth in the city of London in 1792 and who, after a fine education at one of the best schools in the country, entered the world of politics at an early age. By his late twenties he had risen to the position of Aide to the British Ambassador to the United States and his new duties sent him across the Atlantic to Washington DC. There, he met and married my mother, Julia Swann, a second generation American. I, their only child, was born a year later in the summer of 1828. I have very few memories of my early years in America although I do recall that I felt loved and cared for and that as a family we seemed more than happy.

That happiness did not last long, however, as my mother fell ill with scarlet fever when I was four years old and quickly became bedridden and prone to lapses of unconsciousness. I have one vivid memory of sitting by her bed, my mother lying there motionless, her eyes closed, her body slick with sweat, and I remember touching her arm and feeling the heat from it as fiercely as if I had touched a hot coal straight from the fire.

She died the next morning without saying goodbye and I do not remember her funeral.

Soon after my mother's death, my father, heartbroken and lost, returned to London and took a desk job in Westminster. I was sent off to boarding school in the countryside from the age of eight and saw my father maybe three or four times a year until his death from a stroke just before my fifteenth birthday. Suddenly I was alone in the world, yet it somehow felt no different than the previous decade. Having kept myself to myself during my schooling, I had made few friends and instead had come to find comfort in solitude. I had, for many years, expressed myself through my love of art and design and had no intention of following in my late father's footsteps by stepping into the political arena. I decided that a brush and canvas would become my tools, and upon finishing my education I found myself with a decent inheritance and decided to become an artist.

For the next five years I frittered away a vast amount of my inheritance by living beyond my means after finding little success with my paintings. My work was decent, my talent more than the average illustrator or portrait artist, but my style lacked any unique qualities that dealers or collectors desired. Then, by chance, I visited the Great Exhibition of 1851 at the Crystal Palace where a man named Mathew Brady, a photographer, had been awarded a medal for his work. I remember staring at the display of daguerreotype images, of people, buildings, and nature, and I suddenly realised that there was a new way of capturing the beauty (and indeed, the horror) within our world without the use of paints. Yes, in 1851, I found photography - and my calling.

By my twenty-fourth birthday, I had given up my brushes and oils and learnt the basic skills of photography from a few local people who dabbled with such a new medium as this. Over the next several years, I honed my craft by photographing anyone and anything I could, learning new techniques as I worked and reading all I could get my hands on about this almost magical modern invention.

By 1862, having built my business up slowly but surely, and as my reputation grew about the streets of Westminster, I found my services in deep demand from both the poor and affluent alike. But the failed artist in me decided it wanted more. I wanted to make a name for myself. I wanted to be known. So, after learning of Rodger Fenton's famous photographs of the Crimean War taken almost six years before and with a civil war now raging across the Atlantic, I decided to head back to America in pursuit of fame.

My father's name was still a good one and, having inherited from him a politician's 'gift of the gab' and ability to barter a deal (with maybe the help of a few white lies thrown in for good measure), I managed to secure safe transport across the ocean with the help of government and military officials on either shore. Once in Washington DC, I was given permission to travel through Union States, photographing the troops at rest or the or the results of a battle, and I was even given official documentation to carry with me to show I was a civilian that had permission from the highest authorities to perform my duties.

I remained in America from the Spring of '63 until the Autumn of '64 before returning to London without fanfare, a changed man, a troubled man, and that is where my story really starts.

That and the dream, of course.

Yes, the dream – the nightmare - had a lot to do with what unfolded over those few days and nights back in the bleak winter of 1864…

2
NIGHTMARES OF OLD

The dream was this:

It is early dawn when I make a chilling discovery. I am ill, my body still recovering from the fever that had struck me down two nights previous, but the sight that meets my eyes makes any discomfort I feel pale in comparison to the suffering that must have been wrought on the poor souls whose bodies are scattered in front of me.

I dismount my horse. There is a stale-yet-strong scent of smoke in the cool morning air. Putrid and acrid, it mingles with the scent of death that hangs over this place like a shroud. Sickness begins to crawl around my stomach like a venomous snake as I stare at the blood and the gore. I want to look away but cannot tear my eyes from it. In fact, I must capture this! This was why I had travelled here, after all. I had come to record the truth, no matter how ghastly the truth may be.

I hurry to fetch my camera from the mobile darkroom my horse tows behind it when the wind suddenly picks up. Then I freeze, my blood turning cold, as I hear the strange, haunting sound that the wind carries with it...

3
INVITE TO THE CHAMBER OF HORRORS

The knocking at the front door woke me with a start and thankfully saved me from the finale of the nightmare.

I grabbed my pocket-watch from the bedside table and saw that the minute hand was on the eleven and the hour hand was approaching nine. I had recently been sleeping later and later each day and I felt a deep sense of shame as I looked down at the near-empty gin bottle that sat by my bed, knowing that it was to blame. My drinking was becoming less of a habit and more of an addiction that I was constantly making plans to address but had yet to do so, and right then, even so soon after waking, I felt drawn to the bitter mouthful that was left in the bottle, knowing that it would help me face the day ahead.

I instinctively reached for it, but when another set of knocks rapped on the front door, I shrugged the urge away, cleared my throat and called out that I would be one moment.

I pulled on a creased shirt and buttoned it with clumsy fingers before finding a tie and crudely knotting it. Then I dressed in my brown suit, pulled on my shoes, and straightened my greasy hair as I hurried downstairs, hoping that whoever was calling on me would forgive my stubble, tired eyes, and the smell of stale alcohol that no doubt seeped from me.

Bright winter sunlight hit me hard as I pulled open the front door, sending shooting pains into my forehead and causing me to squint. Christmas was only a few days away and the threat of snow had been looming over London for the past week and a heavy frost glistened on the rooftops opposite. As usual, a yellow-tinged smog hung low to the ground, shrouding the man standing on my doorstep.

"Mr Attwood?" he asked, removing his hat, and placing it in front of his chest. He was a short fellow with a stocky build and appeared to be in his mid-to-late thirties. His dark hair was thinning on top but his thick moustache that curled up at the sides was in full bloom and expertly waxed. He too was dressed in a suit, albeit one that looked far more expensive than the one I was wearing.

"Yes, I'm Charles Attwood." I had to clear my throat between the "Yes" and the "I'm" and again I craved a drink to lubricate my throat and rid myself of the hangover that was settling inside of me.

"The photographer?" the man asked, obviously unsure by my decrepit appearance.

"That is" - another cough to clear my dry throat - "correct, sir."

"My name is Jonathon Chambers," he said. "I wish to hire your services."

"You wish for me to take a photograph?" I asked and the smaller man nodded. "Of course, do come inside."

I showed Mr Chambers into the living room which doubled as my work study. My desk and most of my equipment were stored in there and all was in place with no evidence of my addiction (my heaviest drinking was done late on, in my bed, so there was no walking involved when my sight began to fade, and my legs started to weaken). I had been renting this property since my return to England a month earlier and I had not yet had the time to clutter or dirty the place enough to make it shameful. I also had a cleaning lady who came in to tidy and wash for me twice a week and so the two-story terrace looked more than decent to any unexpected visitors. Anyway, I need not have worried about what Mr Chambers thought of my living situation. He did not seem to take any notice of the furnishings or decor but instead looked at several photographs from my collection that hung on the wall above the hearth. The fire was not lit and so he was able to lean in close to study each of them in turn.

"These are very good," he said, stopping in front of a small tintype of a Union solider who had posed for me in Colorado last spring. "I take it you have been out to America?"

"That's correct, sir," I said, not really wanting to think about my time out there but feeling that I had to answer him to be polite.

"My intention had been to capture the reality of conflict and hopefully exhibit the images for the general public back here in England."

Mr Chambers moved along the row of images and stopped at a landscape taken in the Autumn of '63. It showed a field where over one hundred Confederate soldiers and forty Union soldiers had lost their lives only two weeks earlier (although I had deliberately not photographed any of the bodies that had still been there when I had arrived).

"You were very brave to have gone out there, Mr Attwood," he then said. "So very brave."

I knew I was not. I had been greedy, with thoughts of fame and fortune on my mind, and the reason that caused me to leave the U.S so suddenly was added proof of my cowardice. I wanted to change the subject quickly and so I asked him, "You said you required my services?"

When Mr Chambers turned back to me, I noticed for the first time the pain hidden behind his polite smile. His eyes were red, and not just due to the cold weather, and I also noticed by the language of his body, how he held himself with his head low and his shoulders slightly hunched, that he was bearing a mental weight of some kind.

"I hope you do not mind me bothering you without an appointment," he said, "but I have seen you around these last few weeks, mainly down by Westminster Bridge of a weekend."

"Not at all, Mr Chambers. I'm always grateful of any business." Since returning to England, I had made a steady source of income from street photography on Westminster Bridge. Many families out for the day would be tempted to partake in such a modern medium as photography on a whim and the Christmas season had almost doubled my custom as many would send the finished image to family members as a gift. My mobile darkroom was adorned with my name and address and a list of services I provided in the hope of attracting more custom. Fortunately, the good reputation that had preceded me before I had journeyed across the Atlantic was still intact, and even in the space of the last two weeks I had had several clients wishing to hire me for a portrait sitting or to photograph their business premises or a family occasion.

Then there was the other service I offered, one that was in such demand that I had no need to advertise it. For obvious reasons it was my least favourite part of the job, and when Mr Chambers next spoke, his eyes brimmed with tears, his voice cracked with grief, and I knew exactly what he required of me.

"I wish for you to photograph my daughter, Mr Attwood." he said. "She died last night."

4
THE FORMALITIES OF DEATH

Since the invention of photography in its most modern form by Louis Daguerre in France some forty years earlier, post-mortem photography had grown in popularity so much that it was now a common practice amongst all classes of society and certainly when the death was that of a child. It had even evolved from merely photographing a corpse in a coffin to having the deceased in various poses, such as lying on a bed as if asleep or sitting in a chair alongside their living siblings. Sadly, for many grieving parents (certainly poorer ones) that image might be the only photograph they had to remember their child.

"I'm very sorry to hear of your loss," I said as I offered Chambers the most comfortable of the two armchairs.

He wiped his eyes as he took a seat and said, "It was quite sudden. She died during the night. She went to sleep a healthy thirteen-year-old and never woke up." He took a deep breath, as if talking about the death of his daughter was sapping the air from his lungs. "Our doctor examined her body only an hour after we found her. It appears she had died between three and four this morning and he could not find any external signs to suggest anything other than a seizure of some sort. He said he could arrange a post-mortem examination, but my wife and I do not wish for it."

I nodded, assuming that Chambers and his wife were probably practicing Christians who did not agree with the idea of having a loved one cut open after death and put back together before the funeral. In a strange way, I could understand that. After all, finding the cause of death - be it a bad heart, faulty lungs, or a damaged brain - could not bring them back.

"I'm available this morning," I informed him. Today being Sunday I had nothing planned other than an afternoon trip to the bridge to set up my booth and catch some passing trade.

"I am very grateful, Mr Attwood. Thank you." Mr Chambers rubbed his eyes again, dabbing at a tear that threaten to spill down his cheek. "May I ask you something?"

"Of course."

"I have heard of certain techniques that some photographers use when photographing those that have... that have moved on, so that in the finished image the person looks very much alive. Do you practice such techniques?"

I nodded, "I can do, sir, if that's what you wish."

"Yes, that is what my wife and I would want."

"I'd be happy to discuss these things with you and your wife on my arrival. There are various methods I can use to create a lifelike effect."

"Yes, thank you. And let me say now that money is of no object."

That last sentence resonated with me. My trip abroad had cost me a great deal and not having an exhibition on my return had put my finances in a precarious position.

"Shall we say eleven o'clock, Mr Chambers?"

"That would be perfect." He reached into his pocket, pulled out a small card and handed it to me. "My address. My home is not far from here."

I took the card and saw that the address was in one of the wealthiest areas in Westminster.

Yes, I thought. Money *would* be no object.

I showed Mr Chambers outside and offered my condolences once more.

"Thank you," he said. "But if I may be blunt, the most you can offer me is a picture of my little girl as she once was. I would like her to look alive in the finished article."

"Of course," I agreed, and I was confident in my promise.

Mr Chambers bade me goodbye before making his way through the smog and climbing into a two-horse carriage that was parked nearby. The driver of the carriage, a big, burly looking fellow with a thick beard and crooked nose then ushered the two horses away and they happily obliged, trotting off gracefully, pulling the carriage along the street before the smog swallowed them up before they had gone but twenty yards.

I closed the door and set about preparing for my day's work by heading upstairs and drinking what was left in the bottle of gin that sat by my bed.

Recently, it was how I started every day.

5
A SOLEMN APPOINTMENT

After finishing the gin, I headed to the nearby public house, only stopping at a stall to buy the morning *Herald* on my way. I ordered eggs and warm oatmeal bread, and while I waited for the food, I drank a tankard of ale and read the newspaper. The news reports, as usual, were of the morbid kind. There was more political and financial trouble in the ever-growing world; there was a danger of another cholera epidemic due to a failure with the new sewerage system; and there were the usual local crime stories which included the post-office robbery two days ago by two masked men wielding daggers and the arrest and prosecution of a Danish immigrant for the murder of an elderly man last week. That story caught my eye more than the others – not because of the particulars of the case but more so because of a person mentioned in the report.

The murdered man had been a Mr Jeffery Parsons, a retired teacher, who had been found dead in his home several days after his actual murder. After a short police investigation, a local imbecile by the name of Arthur Olsen had been arrested and charged and was due to face the hangman early in the new year. The name of the arresting officer had been what had caught my attention - Detective Inspector Andrew Burke.

I smiled to myself as I finished my drink.

Good old Andrew, I thought. Still working hard. And promoted, too. He had been a sergeant the last time I had seen him. I had known Burke for about seven years, ever since, out of curiosity, he had offered me work on an ad hoc basis with the police force. His idea was that a crime scene could be best documented with the use of a photograph, but alas, after only three jobs together, his superiors did not think my services valid enough and I was made surplus to requirements. Burke and I had stayed friendly, though, and used to often meet up for a drink before I had departed for America. Indeed, besides the people I knew through business needs (iron mongers, pharmacists, and such) I believe Burke was the only friend I had in my adult life.

It was a sad thought, and one which made it easier to order another drink when my breakfast arrived.

The food was bland but filling, and I washed it down with the other ale. Once finished, I stopped at the counter on my way to the door and purchased a bottle of gin to take with me. The barman took my money and handed me a dirty green bottle that was crudely corked, and I looked at it, both lovingly and hatefully, knowing that it would be half empty before I left for Mr Chambers' residence in an hour's time.

I returned home and began drinking it immediately. I told myself I needed it more than usual this morning. The truth was, I was nervous. I had not been hired to photograph a death since before my journey to America. Being around the dead was always uncomfortable but I would have felt less bothered had the deceased been an adult. But this was a child. It *had* to be a child.

Suddenly, somewhere deep inside my mind, I heard the noise from my nightmare, the sound that had been carried on the wind, and so I gulped down more gin to silence it. Very soon, half of the bottle was gone, and I felt as if I could function properly.

I collected some coal and wood from the outside bunker and made a fire in the hearth in my study. Once that was burning nicely and I felt it would warm the house for my return later, I filled a dish with cold water, washed and shaved and then changed into my other suit that was slightly less creased. It was also black and therefore more formal for the occasion. I then gathered what I needed from my study and, in several trips, headed out into the yard at the back of my rented property where my mobile darkroom was located.

The darkroom was a simple cart with added wooden sides, covered with a black canvas top, making it big enough for me to stand up inside and develop the photographic plates without exposing them to light.

I loaded in the two cameras I owned (one for portrait photography that produced a larger image and the other for my street shots), the bottles and jars of chemicals, the iron photographic plates, and the metal pole, clamps, and wooden base block I might need should Mr and Mrs Chambers require their daughter to be photographed in an upright position. Then I went to fetch my horse from the communal stables at the end of the street.

I found Brady munching on his morning hay and he looked up upon hearing my voice, his ears twitching with recognition when he saw me, but that was as far as it went. He had not gotten fully used to me yet as I had only purchased him after arriving back from the U.S after having left my other transport back on the other side of the Atlantic.

I tipped the stableman and then led Brady (who was somewhat grumpy at me for cutting short his breakfast) back to my yard where I attached him to my darkroom. Then we were ready for the off.

The journey only took half an hour, through streets crowded with both the poor and affluent alike. Westminster, although primarily seen as a wealthy part of London, was also home to the infamous 'Devils Acre', where the lowest of the low and worst of the worst lived in abject poverty, meaning that everyday people from all classes mingled and congregated in these parts.

I passed shops and offices with their chimneys spewing thick, black smoke, and market stalls where the aromas of meats and vegetables mixed with the fetid odour of dirty river water from the nearby Thames to create an assault on the senses. With it being the last Sunday before Christmas, there was a more joyous feeling in the air than normal. Children who had escaped the prison of Sunday school crowded in front of shop windows to marvel at toy trains and carved wooden soldiers, and adults studied vast selections of poultry in butcher shops, some wondering what size goose would be big enough for Christmas dinner, others wondering what size bird their meagre wages could afford them. Yes, it was all very festive, and I tried to soak it up as much as possible for I knew that when I arrived at the Chambers' residence all thoughts of Christmas would have been forgotten.

Finally, I pulled up outside a row of modest townhouses in one of the nicer streets in the area. The carriage I had seen Mr Chambers leave in earlier was stationed outside the house directly in the middle of the row and I knew without having to double check the address that this was the property I sought. The curtains were all drawn and on the front door I could see that a wreath had been hung, though obviously not a Christmas decoration. No, this wreath was decorated with black ribbon, signalling to passers-by that a death had occurred inside. A hushed silence seemed to hang over the house as I climbed down from Brady.

I tied the feed bag to the horse's face to keep him occupied while I fixed the brake blocks to the darkroom's back wheels. When I straightened up, the burly driver with the bushy beard and crooked nose was at my side.

"Mr Attwood, sir?" he said, as if there was any doubt (my name and trade were both painted on the side of my cart, remember).

"Yes, here to see Mr Chambers."

"He's expectin' you, sir. Name's Edward." He held out a meaty hand that matched his gruff voice and when I shook it, I could feel the strength it contained. "I work for Mr Chambers. Jobs 'round the house... and I drive for him, too." He thumbed back over his shoulder to the carriage. "I was just cleanin' it and saw you comin'.

"Mr Chambers must be a wealthy man," I said. "May I ask what his profession is?"

Edward nodded. "A solicitor. A good one, too. Self-made man is Mr Chambers. He didn't come from no money background, either. He worked hard, he did. Got himself an education and moved up in the world. Can I give you a hand with your stuff, Mr Attwood?"

I smiled and thanked the big man as I opened the back of the darkroom. I asked him if he would be kind enough to take the metal pole, the clamps, and the wooden base block inside. I would fetch the camera as it was expensive, and I did not trust this friendly brute of a man not to break it.

Mr Chambers came out of the house as Edward and I drew close to the door. He asked if I had found the house alright and I said I had. He thanked me again for agreeing to the job with such short notice and I replied that it was no trouble. He thanked Edward for assisting me and Edward said he was "Glad to help, sir". Then there were a few seconds of silence, as if the tragedy of the situation had settled into the solicitor's soul again. He then nodded to himself, took a deep breath, and said, "Anyway, please do come in," and I did so, stepping over the threshold gingerly.

The hallway was long and narrow with three doors leading off into various rooms. It smelled of hot coal and lavender and was comfortably warm. Directly in front of me were stairs leading up to the first floor and I noticed a housemaid at the top of the flight, busying herself by putting away laundry in a cupboard. She looked down upon hearing the front door close and I noticed her watery eyes and sorrowful expression. Obviously, the death of the child had affected the staff also.

The maid finished what she was doing and moved on to another upstairs room and when she was out of sight, I looked around further. The walls were a dark green and the carpet underfoot was thick and no doubt expensive. Several paintings of country landscapes and portraits of people unknown to me hung on the walls. There were also two oval mirrors that had, in keeping with tradition, been covered with black crape, as those who believed in such things thought it prevented the soul of the deceased from becoming trapped within the glass. To me it was all utter nonsense and superstition but to others it was something important that should be done, like going to church on a Sunday – which I did not.

Mr Chambers asked Edward to take the equipment he carried straight through to the living room and the big man did so, disappearing through the second door on the right before returning quickly and asking if there was anything else he could help with. I said that there was not, and he replied that he would be outside but not to hesitate to call him should we require his services.

I sat my camera down and watched Edward as he left. When I turned back to Mr Chambers, a black figure was suddenly beside him, and because I had heard no one else approach, I am ashamed to say that I almost stepped back in fright.

"Sorry if I startled you," the lady said. She was dressed in black mourning attire and her pale middle-aged face was only just visible behind the veil she wore. Since Prince Albert had died three years earlier and Queen Victoria had taken to only wearing mourning dress in public, the style had become so popular that the sight of women wearing such outfits was common on many London streets throughout the year. Even so, I always felt a shiver of unease upon seeing them. It reminded me that death was always close by. Always ready to strike.

"Of course you did not startle me," I said, feeling my face flush slightly. "No need to apologise, madam."

"This is my wife, Louisa," Mr Chambers said.

I introduced myself and added, "I'm sorry it's under such dire circumstances that we have to meet."

Mrs Chambers nodded and I heard her gently sniff back tears.

"Emily is dressed and ready in the living room," she then said, and I suddenly realised that Mr Chambers had never given his daughter's name.

It was Emily. Emily Chambers. Deceased.

"Is Emily to be photographed alone or...?" I left the question hanging in the air along with the coal and lavender.

Mr Chambers glanced at his wife and then back at me.

"We would like to sit with her," he said, and his voice suddenly became weak with grief. "Despite our financial security we never really had many photographs taken as a family. I suppose, like many others, we assumed there would be many more opportunities." He took one of his wife's hands in one of his own and squeezed, as if grateful he still had one lady in his life. "The first photograph we had taken with Emily was when she was three, ten years ago, with her mother and I sitting either side of her. We would like the last photograph of her to be the same as the first."

I nodded. "Was she sitting or standing in the other photograph?"

"Standing. Will that be a problem?"

"Not at all. The equipment Edward brought in can achieve such an effect. A strong metal pole screwed into a heavy wooden base will form a support frame for a clamp that will hold your daughter's body upright. Another clamp will be fitted around the base of her skull to keep her head up. None of these will be visible on the photograph and none will damage Emily in any way. I hope neither of you will be offended or upset with the use of such equipment."

"Of course not," the solicitor replied, apparently answering for his wife also.

"Good," I said. "One more thing. For a more realistic, life-like image there is the problem of the eyes. May I ask, are Emily's eyes open or closed?"

"They are closed," Mr Chambers told me.

"And I take it that you would want them open?"

"Like I said, Mr Attwood, I wish for her to look alive."

I pulled a sour face and rubbed my head to give the impression that I was considering something. The reality was, I was simply letting Mr and Mrs Chambers think that. I knew what I wanted to do but I wanted them to believe that they had a choice in the matter. For the poorer clients, a simple image would suffice, usually of the body on a bed, and I rarely – if ever – bothered with any of my fancy techniques. But for the more affluent clients where money was no object, I tried to produce the best image as possible and collect as much of a fee as I could.

After a few seconds, I finally nodded and said, "I could try to prop Emily's eyelids open. I have small apparatus that could do such a thing but often the result is a lifeless stare. Another way is to paint realistic pupils onto her closed lids - but I do feel that in some cases they can appear dull and unfocused on the finished photographic plate. My own personal choice is to leave the eyes closed and work on the photographic plate later. I can use oils to paint the pupils directly onto the plate itself. That way I can control the direction in which the eyes will look. Also, if you wish, I could add colour to the plate. I was an artist before I was a photographer and so I can assure both of you that I am confident in my abilities. For example, I could add a very small hint of rouge to Emily's cheeks and lips to give a more healthy and lifelike appearance. I could even add subtle shades to the clothes and background, but the choice is up to your good selves, of course."

I say again, the choice was not theirs really.

Mr Chambers looked at his wife. His wife then looked at me and simply said, "Do what you think is best, Mr Attwood."

I feigned deep thought again.

"Like I told you, my personal preference would be to paint the eyes on later," I said. "But I'm afraid that option is slightly more expensive because of the extra time and work involved."

"Like I have already told you, Mr Attwood, money is no object," Mr Chambers replied without hesitation. "We just want the best result."

"Very well." I stooped to collect my camera. "The living room, you say?"

"Yes," Mr Chambers said, pointing to the door Edward had entered earlier. "We'll show you in."

It was time to meet their daughter.

It was time to meet Emily.

6
MEETING THE DECEASED

Mr Chambers opened the door, and I entered the living room backwards, carrying the camera carefully so that I did not damage it or the door frame. Behind me, I heard the crackling and spitting of a fire. I felt more warmth and the scent of coal and lavender became stronger as I set the camera down next to my other equipment Edward had earlier brought in.

    The room was dim as the curtains were closed but several candles had been lit and placed in various locations to add a little illumination. I noticed another covered mirror above the hearth in which the fire was burning. There was also a bookcase with two vases of flowers either side, a small piano in one corner and, in the other, a grandfather clock with the minute and hour hands having been stopped at three o'clock, to honour of the time of death, I assumed. Lastly, I saw two chairs at the far side of the room. One was empty. In the other was slumped the body of a thirteen-year-old girl.

Emily Chambers' hair was shoulder length and dark in colour, with delicate curls fashioned at its lower lengths. Her face was pale, her complexion as clear as water and her eyes were closed, as if asleep. Upon seeing her for the first time, I could not help but think that she would have grown into an attractive lady had she had the opportunity. She was dressed in a long-sleeved, blood-red dress. It was buttoned up high at the front and the white collar covered most of her neck. It looked expensive and was fashioned from lace and fine cotton. Her arms had been placed on her lap with her hands open slightly. Her thin legs dangled limply under her dress, and she wore black laced-up boots, the tips of which brushed against the carpet, causing her feet to point inwards at awkward angles.

Inside my head, the sound from my nightmare suddenly began again, causing a feeling of dread to churn in my stomach. I had photographed dozens of deceased in my time and almost all of them caused an initial reaction of shock within me. But, because life should never be taken so young, children always caused the greatest reaction, and right then, at that moment, like the hands of the grandfather clock, Emily Chambers had me frozen to the spot.

"Are you alright, Mr Attwood?" Mr Chambers asked and the gut-wrenching sound inside my head suddenly stopped.

I told him that I was, and when it dawned on me that I must have been in the room for over a minute doing nothing but looking around and that it must have appeared strange, I made up a lie and said to him, "I was just checking the light in the room to see if it is suitable."

"And is it?" Mr Chambers asked.

"Yes, if we open the curtains," I said, and Mrs Chambers immediately did just that.

Sunlight flooded in, illuminating Emily more, and I was satisfied it would suffice for the job at hand. It also made the room less sombre, and because of that, I instantly felt a little better.

"Where do you want the photograph taken?" I asked the parents.

"Where the two chairs are," he said. "My wife and I sitting, with Emily standing in-between us."

"Very good," I said. Then, trying to ignore the nearby body of the girl and thinking of a healthy pay packet, I got to work.

Mr and Mrs Chambers watched me in silence as I connected the box camera to its stand and then checked that the mirrors and lenses were in place inside. I then went under the hood and used the viewing holes to position the camera so that Emily and the two chairs almost filled the aperture, and as I did so I tried to ignore the fact that the figure I was looking at was limp and lifeless. Instead, I concentrated on the overall composition of the shot.

All of this was done within a few minutes and alas I could not put off what needed to be done next.

"I'll need you to help me in a moment," I said to Mr Chambers as I collected the pole, clamps and wooden base block and moved between the two chairs, trying not to touch Emily as I did so.

Mr Chambers followed me and asked, "What do you need me to do?"

"I will need you to lift Emily so we can clamp her into an upright position."

"Oh," was all he said.

I placed the wooden block on the floor, in-between the two chairs, towards the back. It was rectangular in shape, two feet long by one foot wide, one foot in height and weighed almost thirty pounds. In the centre was a hole running through it in which I tightly inserted the pole so that it stood up maybe four feet in the air. To the pole's mid-section, I then attached the largest clamp that would be used to grasp Emily's waist and take most of her weight. Finally, a clamp was attached to the top of the central pole to support the dead weight of her skull.

I stepped back, knowing that it was time for the hardest part. I looked at Mr Chambers and said, "Would you lift your daughter please?"

The solicitor stooped and carefully slid his hands between Emily's arms and waist and gently pulled his daughter's body upwards. Her head clumsily slumped against his chest and her arms drooped by her sides as if they were made from lead. Her legs remained straight and rigid, the tips of her feet dragging on the top of the carpet.

"If you could just place her back against the central pole so I may fix the clamp around her waist." I moved behind the chairs and opened the middle clamp to its full capacity. "Please make sure that her feet are flat on the ground. It's important as her legs will also help to support her."

Mr Chambers did so, and I noticed how much heavier Emily must have felt compared to when she had life in her as her father's face showed signs of strain, and so, reluctantly, I took hold of the girl's shoulders to assist him.

The second I touched Emily's body a chill ran through me, and my stomach grew sickly. I fought the urge to shiver to appear as professional as possible as we finally managed to position Emily's back against the central pole. It was not easy.

"Now, please hold her still." I tightened the clamp around the dead girl's waist and as I did so I noticed that Emily smelt strongly of perfume. Even though on a living person the odour would have been pleasant, the sweet, flowery scent almost caused me to gag as in this situation I knew it had been used to mask the smell of death and decay, and it made me hold my breath.

Once Emily was secure, I crouched lower and made sure her legs were straight, her knees locked and her feet flat on the floor in front of the wooden block. Then I stood and gently took hold of both sides of her head and moved it back against the central pole. I again shivered internally at the cold, poultry like touch of her skin as I gently fixed the final clamp around the base of her skull to keep her head upright and facing forward.

Once done, I had broken out into a sweat and so I took my handkerchief out of my breast pocket and dabbed at my face before walking around the chairs to get a front view of my departed subject.

Satisfied she was standing securely and facing forward, I asked Mrs Chambers if she would like to restyle Emily's hair as it had fallen out of place slightly during the positioning of her. As she began to do so, I told both parents, "I shall be back in a couple of minutes. I have to go out to my darkroom and prepare the photographic plate."

I removed the plate holder from my camera and headed outside, glad to escape that sombre room for a few minutes and dreading having to return.

7
MEMENTO MORI

Edward was still cleaning the carriage and must have noticed me leaving, for as I climbed into the back of my cart, disappearing within the black canvas cover, he called, "Is that it done, Mr Attwood? You need help packing up?"

I smiled at his innocence, though from outside he could not see me. "No, thank you, Edward. I've not even started yet."

Inside, in the pitch black of my darkroom, I set up my portable desk and quickly got to work.

I found one of several iron plates I had already cut to size, and I cleaned it with a cloth to make it as shiny as possible. Then I grabbed my bottle of collodion solution (a mixture of pyroxylin, ether, alcohol, and a few other dangerous chemicals a friendly local chemist had prepared for me) and drizzled it onto the centre of the plate. Then, holding the plate firm in one corner, I rotated it until the solution covered the entire surface apart from the tiny corner portion where my fingertips remained. I then tilted the plate and poured any leftover solution back into the bottle. In truth, this could have been performed in the light as the collodion solution was not yet light-sensitive, but I was that used to the process I could have done it blindfolded. However, the next step – sensitising the plate – had to be performed in total darkness.

Holding the plate with metal tongs, I submerged it into a jar of silver nitrate for four minutes. Afterwards, the plate was milky white, sensitive to light and drying by the second. I only had so much time and so I packed it into the camera's plate holder to protect it and quickly carried it back into the house, Edward watching me with curiosity as I did so.

"Now, if you would both please take your positions," I asked the parents as I re-entered the living room and fitted the plate holder back into the camera.

Mr and Mrs Chambers took a seat either side of Emily and sat formally, their hands crossed on their laps, their bodies parallel to each other with Emily seeming to hover between them, her arms hanging limp and useless by her sides. Her pose suddenly appeared very unnatural and the artist in me could not hold back.

Knowing that I could make the composition better, I asked, "Would you mind if I repositioned Emily, slightly?"

"Of course not, Mr Attwood," Mrs Chambers replied. "Do you need help?"

"No, please stay where you are."

I went over and took hold of Emily's right forearm and placed it on the left shoulder of her father so that, with her hand drooping slightly, it appeared that she was casually leaning on him. I then took hold of her left hand and placed it on her mother's right shoulder. I felt Mrs Chambers shudder and hold back more tears as I did this, but I knew she would appreciate the way the pose made Emily appear more natural and lifelike.

"Now, if you are both ready...?" I left the sentence unfinished as I hurried back to the camera. "Please choose a comfortable facial expression. After a count of three, I will start to take the picture and I will require you to keep your face and body as still as possible until I tell you otherwise."

Mrs Chambers held a small, almost painful, smile. Mr Chambers remained straight-faced, trying his best to look proud and dignified.

Emily had no choice but to stay the way I had placed her.

"Good," I said. "One, two three, hold still!"

I removed the dark slide from the camera and took off the lens cap, allowing light onto the photographic plate inside.

Then I slowly counted to five.

It seemed to take forever.

"Done!" I said and snapped the cap back over the front of the camera and slid the dark slide back in place. I then removed the plate holder from the camera and told them, "I shall develop this and see how it has turned out."

"Shall we not...?" Mr Chambers pointed to his daughter, her arm still on his shoulder.

I walked over and gently took hold of Emily's arms and placed them back by her sides.

"You two may stand, if you wish," I told them. "But we better leave Emily the way she is for now. Just in case we need to take another image. I'll be back as quickly as I can."

I hurried back out to my darkroom, ignoring Edward who would no doubt wish to start a conversation with me if I spoke to him first. It was not that I did not like the man, but I had to work alone and in silence for the next several minutes. This was the most dangerous part of my job, and one which had cost many people in my trade (several known to me personally) an early death. The chemicals used in this part could create vapours that could kill a person within minutes and concentration was paramount.

Once inside, back in the dark, I quickly removed the photographic plate from the holder. Everything I needed next was already in place on my desk.

I grabbed the bottle of iron sulphate solution and carefully poured it over the plate, catching the excess with an empty jug underneath.

Slowly, magically, the image began to appear, faint at first, then growing darker the more I poured. After several more seconds Emily and her parents could be seen clearly and I stopped pouring the solution when I thought the tone was at the right levels of dark and light.

Afterwards, and still working quickly, I laid the plate to one side and opened another bottle and poured a solution of potassium cyanide into a shallow dish. Then, using the metal tongs and with a rag tied around my face, I lowered the plate into it so that the picture could be fixed to the metal surface. I instinctively took shallow breaths to avoid inhaling much of the bitter fumes of the chemical, knowing that they were potentially life-threatening if one was to be overcome by them.

Once I knew the image was fixed firmly, I removed the plate and then poured the cyanide solution back into the bottle and sealed the lid tight. All that was left to do now was wash the plate with clean water, which I did using water from another bottle and letting it drain off into another empty dish. Finally, I dried it and took it outside into the light to check the quality. I found that it was good. Later, after I worked on it a little with my paints, I knew it would be perfect.

Satisfied, I made my way back into the house and showed Mr and Mrs Chambers the image when they met me at the living room door.

"It looks beautiful," Mrs Chambers said, dabbing at her eyes with a tissue. "*Emily* looks beautiful."

"She'll look even more so after I have added her eyes and some colour."

"So, we do not need to sit for another photograph?" Mr Chambers asked.

"No." I looked across the room at Emily, still upright, a standing corpse. "We can take her down now."

Mr Chambers turned to his wife and told her, "Let Mr Attwood and I finish up here, Louisa. Why do you not go and ask April to make us some tea?"

"Of course," she said and did not look back at Emily as she left the room, as if the sight of her daughter still standing artificially was finally too much to bear.

I placed the photograph in a leather case I kept with me to keep it safe until I got home and could work on it more. Then Mr Chambers and I turned our attention to Emily, working the opposite way than we had earlier.

I disconnected the clamp from the base of her skull and her head lolled forward against her father's chest as he supported her weight. I then undid the clamp from around her waist and the two of us helped her back into the chair her mother had been sat on a few minutes earlier.

When we had finished, Mr Chambers stared at his daughter again, appearing lost in his own dark and morbid thoughts.

"The undertaker has already been and measured her," he then said, out of nowhere. "Her coffin is being delivered tomorrow. It all seems so final now. My beloved Emily is gone."

I really did not know what to say, so I said nothing as I quickly disconnected my camera from its stand, gathered my equipment and placed them by the door. My work here was done, and I was relieved when Mr Chambers snapped from his trance and said he would call Edward to help me load it all back into my cart. I was not, however, expecting him to exit the room so suddenly and leave me in there alone, and when he did just that, the temperature seemed to drop by several degrees and a rush of cold air down the chimney made the fire roar and spit, causing me to jump.

I took one last look at Emily Chambers slumped in the chair, at the sad waste of such a young life, a life taken so suddenly and unexpectedly, and the haunting sound from my nightmare returned to me again, growing louder and louder inside my head until I thought I could take it no more.

When Edward entered the room a moment later, I swear I had never been more grateful for company in all my life.

8
WORDS OF WARNING

I politely refused Mrs Chambers' offer of a cup of tea and I also refused payment there and then from her husband, informing him that I would only accept my fee once the photograph was fully complete. I would have it ready by the morning and would be happy to deliver the finished article to him personally. He thanked me and we agreed on the hour of eleven the next day and the two of us shook hands.

Mr Chambers then saw me outside and waited at the door as I headed to where Edward was loading the rest of my equipment into the cart. It was then that I noticed a young lady standing at the corner of the street. She was dressed in a long grey coat and wore a large, wide-brimmed hat of the same colour. Her hands, covered with fingerless, dainty white gloves, held a small umbrella above her head to keep the winter sun from her eyes. She was staring over towards the house.

I turned back and briefly caught Mr Chambers looking back at her before he suddenly went inside and closed the door to the outside world. The lady then glanced at my darkroom, as if reading the words on the side of it, and then quickly walked out of sight behind the next row of houses.

I loaded my camera inside the cart and closed the back of it. Then I asked Edward if he knew who the woman was.

"Woman, Mr Attwood?" he asked. "What woman?"

I pointed to where she had been, only maybe fifty yards to the left of him, and asked, "She was just there. Did you not see her? She was looking at the house."

Edward peered round the side of my darkroom at the now deserted part of the street where I was pointing. "Over there you say, Mr Attwood?"

"Yes, right there."

"No wonder I didn't see her." He pointed to his left eye. "Illness when I was a little one. Caught a fever and lost most of the sight in it. Still, least I survived. Got to be grateful for that, I have." He loaded the rest of my equipment and shut the back of the cart. "I don't know who you might be talkin' about, though, Mr Attwood. Probably just a neighbour payin' her respects."

I nodded. Yes, maybe Edward was right.

We shook hands and he helped me undo the brakes on the cart. Then, after readying Brady, I set off towards Westminster Bridge and the opportunity to make a little more money.

*

Many families were out enjoying the crisp, December weather and within five minutes of my arrival I had my first customers as several others gathered around to watch before maybe deciding to have a photograph taken for themselves.

The process for each one took less than ten minutes. Priming and sensitizing the iron plates (which were half the size I had used for Emily's picture) took five minutes or so. The actual picture taking (including positioning the sitters) took about a minute. The development and fixing in my dark cart and then placing the photograph in the readied cardboard sleeve about another two or three minutes. Then I was onto the next one.

By the time I got to my eighth or ninth customer I was well into my routine. After handing over a finished product and accepting payment I would then tell the next customers that I would be back in a minute and head inside my darkroom to prepare the next plate. At this stage, being very aware of how much business I was doing, I barely even looked at them when I spoke. That was why I was taken by surprise when I told the next gentleman to excuse me for a moment and he replied with, "After only two years you don't recognise me?"

I stopped and turned upon hearing the voice. The man looked a year or two older than me, taller and strong looking, his face round and well fed beneath the smart bowler hat he wore. His suit was grey and pressed to precision. The lady to his right was dressed elegantly and graceful in her Sunday best with a fashionable hat decorated with pink roses. The two twin boys by her side were smart and impish in their matching jackets and short trousers.

"Andrew!" I said and offered my hand.

"Good to see you again, Charlie-boy," detective Burke said.

"Good to see you, too, my friend." I turned to his wife. "Diana, you look as beautiful as ever."

She feigned shyness and said, "And you're just as charming as ever. You remember the twins, don't you?"

I looked down at the boys, both golden haired and faces full of freckles. "Yes. Jacob and Jeremy. My goodness, you two were no more than infants the last I saw of you."

"They turned seven last month," Burke said. "Both strong and healthy boys." He ruffled the hair on their heads before turning back to me. "I'll not keep you from your work because I can see that you're busy. But how long have you been back?"

"Just under a month," I told him.

"And how was America?"

I smiled, trying to push away the painful memories and waiting for the sound from my nightmare to come again.

Thankfully, this time it did not.

"Remember the night I told you that I was planning to travel there and photograph the civil war, and you said that I was mad, and that it would be the toughest and most dangerous thing I ever did?"

"I do."

"You were right."

Burke laughed and slapped my shoulder. "Well, at least you came back in one piece, Charlie-boy."

I nodded, but not in agreement, and had Burke not spoken again I was sure the sound would then have started in my head as a reminder.

"Well, like I say, I don't want to keep you from your work. I just wanted to stop by and offer a quick hello, but maybe we should meet up sometime. Catch up with what's been happening." He looked at my darkroom. At my address. "I see you're living in New Wood Street now."

"Yes, I've rented a place there. Are still over in Horseferry Road?"

"No," Burke said. "We moved to a bigger house last year as the boys were getting too big to share a room with us." He ruffled the twins' hair again and they both giggled. "So, you live near the Iron Horse pub."

"Yes. That's where I've been having most of my meals."

"That'll put you in more danger than any war ever would," Burke said, and I laughed, knowing that the food there was not the best and that a lot of the clientele did not come from some of the better families that inhabited the area. "How about we meet up there then? Today is my day with my family, but how about tomorrow, after my shift? Say, six o'clock."

"Agreed." I shook his hand. "I'll see you then."

"Until then, Charlie-boy." Burke looked at my customers one last time. "And with business this good, you can buy the drinks."

That said, he and his family moved on. I waved to the children and they waved back. Then I turned to the lady who next approached me and was about to explain that I had to prepare the next photographic plate before I could do business with her when she interrupted by saying, "I am not here to be photographed either, Mr Attwood."

I sighed. It appeared that my friend Burke had started a trend. Then recognition set in, and I realised that she was the lady with the umbrella that I had seen when leaving the Chambers' residence. However, earlier I had not noticed how pretty she was. I assumed her to be maybe three or four years younger than myself, which would place her in her early thirties. Her eyes were large, the lashes long and dark. Her nose was petite, her lips full and feminine and the long coat and dress she wore did little to hide a womanly figure that would turn many a red-blooded man's head.

"If you don't wish to be photographed then how may I help you?"

"Was it a child?" she asked, her voice soft, her words well pronounced.

I frowned, confused by her question. "Who?"

"The person you photographed?" she asked. "The one who died?"

"Are you speaking of Emily?"

"Was she Mr Chambers' daughter?"

"Yes."

The lady lowered her head, as if saddened but not surprised by my answer.

"Was her death due to illness or injury?" she then asked.

"I don't think it's my place to divulge such sensitive information," I said, flashing her a tight-lipped smile and holding up my hands, as if to show her that I had no choice but to answer that way and that I was not deliberately being rude. Then, realising that answering this simple question might hurry her along and let me get back to work, I reluctantly said, "Not that I'm aware of."

"Do you know if there was a flower found with her body?" she then asked.

"A what?" I asked.

"A lily?"

"I don't understand..."

"Did someone leave a lily on her body?"

"Why would they?"

"To show why she had died."

I was suddenly totally lost with what this lady was talking about.

"What do you mean, to show *why* she died?" I asked. "Her father said she died suddenly in her sleep. Nothing more than that."

"That is what they said about Adam," the lady said, and before I could ask who Adam was, she added, "Mr Attwood, her father did not listen to me but maybe he will listen to you-"

"Look, I really have to get back to work," I interrupted.

"That girl did not simply die in her sleep," the lady went on, ignoring me. "I know it and her father knows it, only I am not scared to say so. Emily Chambers was killed."

I cocked my head, like a person might upon hearing a strange sound at night. "You mean, murdered?"

"I do, sir."

I suddenly had no more time for this.

"Look, Miss...?"

"Hunter. Mary Hunter," she said.

"...Miss Hunter, I'm trying to work. I've no idea what you are talking about and I'm very busy. This is none of my business. If you have concerns about Emily Chambers, then maybe you should take them up with her father."

"I spoke to him just over a week ago," she said. "I showed him what I had discovered, but he acted like it was all nonsense and now his daughter has paid the price. Won't you help me?"

Her words hung in the air for a few seconds before I shrugged them away.

"No," I told her. Then, more sternly, I added, "Now, leave me be."

Miss Hunter shook her head in defeat. Then she looked at the photographic plate I held and said, "Then for your sake, I hope Emily's spirit is not angry with you for taking her photograph."

I rolled my eyes. This was not the first time I had heard such a thing. A lot of people believed that photographing the deceased stopped their soul or spirit from moving on to the next life, just like they believed the nonsense and lies spouted by the so-called mediums at these new-fangled seances that were all the rage these days.

"Her spirit has no say in the matter," I said, "for I do not believe in such things."

Miss Hunter remained straight-faced, like my beliefs did not matter in the least, as she said, "Maybe you should, Mr Attwood."

I dismissed her with a wave of my hand and headed into my darkroom to prepare the next photographic plate. The poor woman was delusional with all her talk of murder and spirits, and I decided I would not concern myself with the ramblings of a crazy person any longer.

When I came back outside, Miss Hunter had gone, so I got back to work and tried to think no more of her.

It was not easy.

9
BRINGING BACK THE DEAD

I left Westminster Bridge at half three, when dusk began to settle in fast, and the cold began to nip like sharpened teeth. After parking the mobile darkroom in the yard behind my house and carrying my equipment into the study, I took the unfinished photograph of Emily Chambers out of the leather case and spent a few seconds studying her image, feeling a mixture of sadness and inspiration as I made plans on how to bring her to life with the use of simple oil paints. Also, I could not help but think more about this deceased girl than any of the others I had photographed over the years as her sudden death and the strange behaviour of Miss Hunter still disturbed me somewhat. I had found most of this day quite surreal and I also knew that now night was descending, my feeling of unease would increase. But I had a job to finish and a payment to collect in the morning.

First though I needed to eat and then buy my supplies for the night.

I walked Brady to the stables and afterwards made my way to The Iron Horse on foot for my last meal of the day. By five I had eaten a fair meal of lamb and vegetables and followed it by drinking several ales whilst enjoying my tobacco at a table by myself. Miss Hunter still dominated my thoughts, though. How strange she had been. But then there were a lot of strange characters about these days. 'The Devil's Acre' was testament to that with their prostitutes and criminals and thugs, as were the numerous asylums that had sprung up in recent years. The poor woman was probably suffering from some form of mental ailment, and I briefly considered mentioning her to Mr Chambers in the morning but quickly decided against it. He had been through enough and I did not need to encroach on his grief with such talk. Anyway, none of this was really anything to do with me. All I had to do was finish the photograph and collect my fee.

And time was getting on.

Finally satisfied with what I had eaten and smoked, I bought two bottles of gin from the bar and left the pub. The streets were dark and quiet, the weather now freezing. The wind had also picked up somewhat, tossing litter and bad smells around the alleyways and narrow streets and I was glad of the warmth as I stepped into my study by the stroke of six.

I threw more coal on the downstairs fire and then headed upstairs and made up the one in the bedroom for later. Then the first bottle of gin was opened and a quarter of it was gone by the time I sat down at my desk to begin work on Emily's photograph fifteen minutes later.

I took a cloth and wiped the iron plate carefully, making sure it was totally dirt and fingerprint free. When I had finished, the picture was crisp, the blacks stark and bold, the lighter areas clear and bright, and again I was suddenly struck by the tragic image of the innocent youth who had been taken way before her time. There she was, Emily Chambers, positioned in place by poles and clamps, now waiting for me to add even more fake life to her with the use of paints. Even when finished, I knew that to my eyes at least, the illusion would never be complete. Despite the weak smile of her mother and her father's strong expression, the trauma was etched into their eyes and was impossible for me not to notice. This was no usual, happy family portrait, and none of my magic could mask that.

Miss Hunter's voice suddenly echoed in my head.

"Emily Chambers was killed..."

I shrugged her words away and concentrated on the job at hand.

With my tray of utensils beside me, I decided, as always, to work on the background colours first. I would add a little blue to the curtains behind the three figures and maybe a little faint yellow to the walls either side, just to brighten the overall composition.

I prepared some colours on a palette and diluted them with turpentine so as the liquid consistency would allow some of the darker shades from the photograph to show through. Then, looking through the magnifying glass on the stand next to me to enlarge the image, I dipped a small brush into the first mix of colour and went to work.

I added a thin layer of darkened ultramarine to the curtains and then a cadmium yellow to the walls and was happy with the results. The colours were indeed subtle, so subtle that one with less than perfect eyesight might miss them, but even if consciously unnoticed they gave an extra dimension to the overall picture. I then added a soft purple to each of the chairs, to give the appearance of soft velvet.

Then, I turned my attention to the three figures.

To Mr Chambers' suit, I added a pale brown, which worked well and gave the effect of fine cotton. I left Mrs Chambers' outfit untouched as the black of her dress was unable to be changed for the better, but I did add a striking red to Emily's dress, which the shadows from the photograph showed through, enhancing the folds of the cloth and the shape of her legs beneath.

Satisfied, I took a break, lit a pipe, and drank several coarse mouthfuls of gin. Outside, despite the cold and the wind, in the street somewhere, a group of carollers started up. 'The First Noel' was their first song and I happily listened for a moment before getting back to work.

I gently heated the photographic plate over a candle flame to speed up the paint drying process, moving it constantly to avoid the image melting or bubbling in any places, and once it was dry, I began the second phase.

I added a light peach pigment to each face and hand. To Emily, with the aid of a single-hair brush, I added rouge to the cheeks and mouth and then heated the plate again.

Outside, the carollers moved on to 'Silent Night'.

Finally, it was time for the eyes.

I cleaned the single-hair brush and mixed some dark brown, the colour I assumed Emily's eyes had been, judging by her hair colour. As I leaned in close to the magnifying glass and steadied my hand, the wind outside suddenly picked up and the fire roared in the hearth, the flames fanned by the cold air being pushed down the chimney.

The sound of 'Silent Night' in the background faded out and, in its place, came the sound from my nightmare once more.

The sound of a child.

The sound of crying.

I froze, the tip of the brush about to touch the photographic plate.

Suddenly, I felt uneasy about bringing Emily to false life. It did not seem right. It seemed like a was trying to play God, although no doubt it was simply a combination of the dark night and the lingering words of Miss Hunter making me nervous.

"I hope Emily's spirit is not angry with you..."

Hogwash! I soon told myself. I had learned long ago not to believe in superstitions. If the spirits of the dead sometimes remained behind on this earth, then surely there would be some definitive proof in a day and age of science and industrial progress such as this. Even during this early age of the photograph, no spirit had ever been captured – despite several claims by both photographers and mediums to the contrary. I had seen many fakes (people wearing masks and dressed in bedclothes) and had even produced effective images myself due to mishaps that had created translucent figures that looked of another world, but I had not captured anything I could not explain and therefore did not believe in spirit photography or, indeed, the afterlife itself.

Yes, it was hogwash, and as soon as I thought this, the sound of the crying child ceased, and the carols began again.

I went to work on Emily's eyes without a second pause, gently applying the colour smoothly. Then I added a solid dot of black in the centre of each to form the pupil. Afterwards, all I had to do was wait until that coat had dried and then add a speck of white to give the impression of a reflection in healthy, child-like eyes.

So, I waited.

And while I waited, I drank, and while I drank, I stared at Emily Chambers, who almost stared back. Outside, the wind howled from time to time and the fire roared. Soon the carols stopped for the night. It was getting late.

The first bottle of gin gone and tiredness overcoming me as the time approached nine o'clock, I finished Emily's eyes with one touch of white in each, the position and angle of the fake reflection mirroring those in her parents' eyes.

The illusion was complete.

I gave the photographic plate one last, short heat above the candle flame. Then, finally, for presentation, I encased it in a wooden frame with a glass front, which I cleaned and polished so it sparkled like new.

By nine-thirty it was finished, and I was proud of my work.

I had brought Emily Chambers back to life as much as any man could.

10
EMILY?

I retired to my bedroom where I stripped into my underclothes. Soon, I was sat in bed, sipping from the second bottle of gin, with the crumpled newspaper I had purchased that morning on my lap (which was the only available reading material to occupy my mind until drunken oblivion claimed me like it had done every night recently).

I re-read about the worry of another outbreak of disease, the murder that my friend Burke had helped solve, unrest in politics, and other doom and gloom that seemed the norm these days. All the while my thoughts were elsewhere, though. They were with Mr and Mrs Chambers, and wondering how they felt right now, going to bed for the first time with the death of their daughter fresh in their minds. I thought about what they had to face in the coming days, of a funeral and of saying goodbye and of an empty child's bedroom in their plush house. I thought about Miss Hunter and her crazy stories. I thought about Emily and how she had died. Had she been aware of what was happening to her as the seizure struck? Did she wake in pain and terror or remain sleeping as her life was snuffed out like a candle flame caught in a breeze? I thought all of this and more until my thoughts started to fog and my head started to spin and feel heavy.

By ten o'clock, I placed the near-empty bottle by the side of my bed, lay back, and pulled the covers over me, hoping I would not dream, but certain that I would.

*

I knew nothing for several peaceful hours but when I did wake, I did so with a start, sitting up in bed, my heart racing and my palms sweating.

I was not sure of where I was at first, as was usual upon waking after a night of heavy drinking. Looking toward the window, I saw that it was pitch black outside and eerily quiet, the strong wind having blown itself out, and so I assumed that it must be the early hours of the morning. Also, the nightmare had not yet troubled me, and it had an unwavering habit of occurring at the very end of my night's rest. So, still curious of the time, I rolled over and grabbed my watch from the table.

It was a just after three in the morning.

My head still groggy from what I had consumed earlier and tiredness clawing at my eyes with jagged nails, I fluffed up my pillow and tried to make myself comfortable when I heard a noise downstairs.

It was not a strange noise, nor sinister. Just a single thud of something hitting the floorboards downstairs somewhere, and indeed had it occurred during the hours of daylight, I would have felt no fear in investigating the source and simply finding that something had fallen over due to being precariously balanced. However, this was not daylight, and my mind was still swirling with images of dead children and tales of murder and spirits, and so the sound did indeed send shivers down my spine and froze me still, my eyes wide like those of a startled deer that has heard the approach of the huntsman.

It is just the pole I had used to support Emily's body falling over in my study, I told myself. *It has rolled against the wall which I had propped it and clattered to the floor-*

But then the noise came again, and this time it did not sound like something had fallen, but rather that something heavy was being dragged across the floorboards, or that someone large and wearing boots was slowly walking about down there, dragging their feet as they went.

Someone is in the house!

Terrified but determined to protect my property, I slid out of bed and reached behind the table for the iron bar that I kept there. Although I did not live in one of the poorer areas of the city, there were no real safe places in London. Less than a mile from my house a lot of people were desperate and starving, and so were their neighbours, and therefore the more privileged areas were a hot bed for crime. I had money in my bedroom. I had expensive equipment downstairs. They would not have them!

With my bare feet slapping against the warm floorboards, I inched past the hearth and the smouldering coals in the dying fire. When I reached the bedroom door, I pulled it open quickly so that it made a noise. Indeed, I hoped whoever was downstairs would hear me and quickly make their escape whichever way they had come in. But then I had a second thought, a terrifying one: what if they heard the door and came up and attacked me and took what they had come for anyway?

I immediately cursed my foolishness but remained where I was. I had made my move and had no choice but to investigate further. So, I went out onto the landing.

The top of the staircase was only a few feet from my bedroom door, and I craned my neck and looked down the flight to the hallway, but it was too dark to see anything.

"Who's there!" I demanded and was answered by a deafening silence. "I warn you, you had better leave right now!"

Again, everything was quiet, and just as my nerves began to settle and I was about to blame the gin for my foolishness, the noise came again.

Thud!

Nervously, I raced back to my bedside table and lit a candle with shaking hands and placed it into the holder. The flame cast a warm, eerie glow about the room and made fleeting shadows across the walls that formed strange and sinister shapes as I edged slowly back to the door and out onto the landing once more.

Holding the iron bar aloft in one hand and the candle holder in front of me with the other, I took a deep breath and descended the stairs gingerly, allowing the light to illuminate the hallway the closer I got. The front door was closed shut and I checked the handle when I reached it. It was locked. Then the noise came again, from behind the closed door to my study. I gripped the metal bar tighter as I approached it, the flickering of the candle's flame again playing tricks with my eyes, making the shadows it cast on the walls look like figures from Hell.

I swallowed hard and pushed the study door open, its creaking sending cold, tickling fingers down my neck and causing my hair to stand on end, like that of a dog that has been threatened.

Despite my fear, I rushed inside.

Of course, there was no one in the study. My equipment was stacked neatly in one corner. My paints were still by my desk. The photograph of Emily Chambers and her parents was where I had left it, untouched. The only noise was the odd spit or crackle of the dying fire in the hearth. Everything was the way it should be.

I placed the candle on the desk and rubbed my face, feeling foolish but giddy with relief, and with the relief came tiredness again.

Today has gotten to you, Charles, I told myself. *And the gin is not helping...*

Ready to return to bed, I reached for the candle and saw that something was suddenly next to my hand, and that is when my heart leaped into my throat and the strength was instantly sapped from my legs.

Despite the shock that was settling into my bones, I managed to pull the seat out from under the desk and slump down into it to save me collapsing to the floor.

The flickering candlelight was illuminating something on my desk, something that should not have been there, something that had never been there before.

A flower. A single white lily.

I did not need to touch it to know that it was real as I could smell its sweet and potent scent from where I sat. Then, just as my eyes had been drawn to it, they were soon drawn to the photograph of the Chambers family close by.

I dropped the iron bar I had been carrying and did not even jump as it clanged to the floorboards. My eyes never left the photograph, and without thinking I reached for it and pulled it close to my face to take a better look.

What the...?

Both Mr and Mrs Chambers were sat in the chairs, facing the camera, as expected. But the space between them, the space where Emily had been positioned, was empty - no, not empty exactly, for the shape of her body could still be discerned, but instead of seeing her face and her blood-red dress and her arms resting on her parents' shoulders, all that could be seen was the dull metal of the photographic plate.

I blinked rapidly and shook my head, as if to get my brain working, for it had surely cheated me.

I looked again and saw that I had not been mistaken.

Emily Chambers had somehow escaped the picture.

Then the noise came again. This time behind me. It was a thud followed by a dull scrape, as if something of considerable weight was dragging itself closer to me, and I stiffened, my body going rigid, not wanting to turn and look, for I had a notion of what I would see should I do so.

Emily! It's Emily, dragging herself towards me, the pole and heavy base block weighing her down, slowing her movements...

A familiar scent suddenly filled the room, sweet and sickly and I recognised it as the perfume that had been on the child when I had photographed her.

Oh, my God! It is her! Dragging herself closer to me...

Sitting rigid in the chair and daring not to turn around, I imagined the poor girl, stiff and awkward, her eyes closed, her body pale and dead, creeping in an almost somnambulistic manner upon me. Me! Her creator! The one who had brought her back from the other side!

"For your sake, I hope Emily's spirit is not angry..."

Suddenly, the noise was right behind me, at the back of my chair and I swear I felt cold, dead breath on the nape of my neck, followed by a voice, one which may once have been soft and childlike, but which death had now rendered hoarse and dry.

"Help me..." it said.

Outside, the wind suddenly picked up. What was left of the fire and the flame in the candle both died out, plunging the room into absolute, impenetrable darkness.

"Please, help me..."

It was then that I believe I screamed.

11
THE COLD LIGHT OF DAY

I try settling my horse as the sound drifts towards me, knowing that I must be wrong, that I could not possibly be hearing what I think I am.

I remind myself that I am standing amongst the remnants of a slaughter, a massacre, and that everyone around me is surely very dead and beyond all hope. What I hear is imaginary. It must be. Surely the sickness I am recovering from is affecting my ability to think straight and I am still a little delirious.

But the sound of crying continues.

I look towards where I believe it to be originating, beyond the other side of a smouldering tent where several bodies lie scattered about, their clothes either torn and ripped, or removed entirely to reveal bloody wounds and innards that have burst free and glisten in the sunlight. Some are missing limbs. Others are missing more sensitive body parts. At least most of the bodies are those of women and children.

Without thinking, I slowly walk closer to where I believe the crying to be emanating from, and as I approach the partially clothed body of a young Indian woman, the crying suddenly becomes more of a scream...

The next thing I knew was that I was waking up at my desk in the study and it was light outside, the sound of traffic and voices from the other side of the window bringing me instant comfort.

I sat up quickly, my head still swimming, my mind still half asleep, and looked around the room as if I had suddenly found myself in the strangest place. The usual nightmare was still fresh in my mind and I tried hard to push it back and remember what had come before it. I then saw the candle on the desk and my bare feet kicked against the iron bar on the floor.

Slowly, the events of the previous night returned to me.

I had heard a noise and thinking it was an intruder had come down to investigate. But there had been no intruder, so what had I heard?

Then I remembered and reached for the photograph.

Emily! I had heard Emily! She had been missing from the photograph!

I stared at the iron plate inside the wooden case and glass frame and of course it was as normal as it should have been, the three figures captured forever inside by a mixture of chemicals and light. And the flower that had been on my desk?

I looked and could not see any trace of it.

Then why had I imagined...?

Suddenly, from the hallway, I heard the front door open, followed by footsteps and the sound of a woman happily humming a Christmas hymn.

"The holly and the ivy, when they are both full grown..."

Unlike last night, however, this was not an unexpected visitor. Neither was it imagined, as I now tried to convince myself that what I had witnessed must have been as

I headed out to the hall to greet my cleaning lady.

Miss Dawson came in to tidy and wash for me on Mondays and again on Tuesdays to return my fresh clothes and linen that she thankfully took away to iron overnight. She was a short, painfully thin lady in her late forties who was not unattractive but who's hard life had aged her greatly. She had no husband or family that I knew of and she had to fend for herself by offering her services to the wealthier households in the area, being paid by the job so that she could afford a roof over her head each night.

Obviously expecting me to be either upstairs or out already, the small lady jumped and squealed as she heard the study door open behind her as she fiddled with her sweeping brush and bucket of rags and cloths.

"Oh, Mr Attwood!" She gasped when she saw it was me and placed a hand on her chest. She then blushed when she noticed I was still in my nightwear. "Sorry, I didn't know you weren't decent. I didn't think you'd be in, sir. You gave me a start."

I apologised and said, "I'm always in at this time." Then I realised I had no idea what time it was. "What time is it?"

Miss Dawson did not look at a watch but said, "It's just gone ten, sir. That's why I thought you would be out for breakfast by now and so I used the spare key you gave me. I know I'm usually here around nine but there was extra work for me at the Gladstone's a few doors up and, well, money is money. I hope you don't mind me being late, Mr Attwood?"

"Not at all," I said, but was too busy thinking about the time. *After ten?* I said I would be at Mr Chambers' residence by eleven. I had better get a move on.

And you had better lay off the gin also! It's ruining you...

"You been up all night working, sir?" my housekeeper then asked.

I looked back at the study, the door slowly closing behind me. "Erm, yes."

"Did you have an important job to finish, Mr Attwood?"

I could not help smiling at Miss Dawson's enquiries. From the day she introduced herself to offer her services she seemed very sweet but talkative to the point of meddling.

"I had to finish something for a client," I told her.

"May I see it, sir?" she asked. "You know how I've always been amazed by those photography things."

"You know I usually would, Miss Dawson, but I am afraid this one is of a very sensitive nature." I lowered my head slightly, as if paying respect at a funeral.

Her eyes widened, as if she understood what I meant. "Oh, I'm sorry, sir. One of *them* ones, is it? I know a lot of people is getting them done when a loved one passes on – 'specially where I live and 'specially children. In fact, just last week a friend of a friend of mine lost her son to a fever. He was only two years old. She had to take his little body round to a camera man's house to get *his* picture took."

"That's a shame," I said on my way to the stairs. I was not being heartless, I just really needed to get dressed. Also, I did not really want to hear about more dead children right now. I had enough on my mind.

Why had I imagined Emily last night? Why had she pleaded for help? Was this the start of more torment? Was this another nightmare child to plague me during my hours of rest?

"It is, sir," Miss Dawson said, and I was taken aback, lost with the conversation.

"I'm sorry?"

"I said it *is* a shame. Pity I never knew of the boy's death at the time or I could have recommended your good self. Not many camera people have one of those horse-drawn things like you."

"Mobile darkroom," I corrected her.

"Yes, sir. You could have come to her and saved her a heartache of a trip."

I agreed that I could have and then politely told her that I had things to do. My housekeeper apologised and said she would let me go, but not before telling me that if she heard of any more deaths that required my services then she would put a word in for me.

I thanked her and headed back to my bedroom to dress and to try to make sense of what had happened last night.

Eventually, with the help of my leftover gin, I decided that the answer was a simple one. I had fallen asleep inebriated, my mind still focused on Miss Hunter's strange behaviour and the macabre memory of photographing Emily. A noise (something falling over, or the house settling, or something in my imagination) had woken me, dragging me from sleep prematurely so that I was not fully awake and possible still a little drunk. With my brain not functioning properly, I had sleepwalked somehow to my study where the late hour, tiredness and alcohol had made me imagine the flower and the young girl escaping from the photograph. Then I had fallen back into a true sleep at my desk.

Yes, simple, and it all seemed rather foolish now that I thought back to it in the cold light of day, with Miss Dawson cheerfully pottering about downstairs.

But why was Emily asking for help?

That, I could not answer. But time was getting on and I could not waste any more of it thinking about such things.

I dressed and collected my equipment and loaded up my cart. I then fetched Brady and readied him for the journey. Finally, I went back inside and paid Miss Dawson for her morning's work and told her I would see her tomorrow.

"Oh, yes, Mr Attwood," she said, on her hands and knees as she scrubbed the kitchen floor. "You will. I'll try and be a little earlier tomorrow."

I bade her farewell and then collected Emily's photograph from the study.

Remember, it was only your imagination, I told myself as I wrapped it in brown paper and tied it tight with string. *You will soon forget about it.*

As I left for my day's work, I assured myself that this would be the last I ever thought about Emily Chambers.

But, alas, I had been wrong before...

12
A SECOND INVITE

I rode to Mr Chambers' house through weather that was crisp and bright but with dark clouds gathering on the horizon. My mood was very much like the sky. I was on my way to collect a decent pay – more than I would make in two Sunday afternoons by the river – and I was happy at the prospect. But the events of the previous night still lurked in my mind, as dark and depressing as the clouds in the distance, and all I could do was hope that they would eventually pass and cause me no trouble.

I saw Edward sitting in the carriage's driver's seat that was parked outside of the house again, possibly waiting to take Mr Chamber's somewhere or having just returned with him for us to complete our business and waiting there to take him somewhere else after I left. I assumed Mr Chambers had a lot to do, and none of it involving his profession as a solicitor. He had a funeral to prepare for. He would have to contact those he wished to attend. He would have to arrange flowers and transport and several other things he had never planned or wanted to do.

Edward looked over at me as I climbed down from Brady, and a moment later I approached him on my way to the house.

"Good morning," I greeted him.

"Ah, Mr Attwood, sir." He leaned down from the driver's seat and shook my hand. "Come with the photograph, have you?"

I raised the package I carried and nodded. "Is Mr Chambers home?"

"He is. We've been out early this mornin'. Things to do, unfortunately. But he wanted to be back for you comin'. Didn't want his good lady wife to deal with it by herself. Here, I'll show you in."

Edward made to climb down from the carriage, but I stopped him and said, "No, don't bother yourself. I'll ring the doorbell."

Edward looked from me to the house and then finally back at me. He nodded. "Very well, Mr Attwood."

I began to walk away but then, out of nowhere (I was not thinking of her, I swear,) I heard Emily's ghostly voice in my head.

(Help me...)

I stopped in my tracks, like someone who has just realised they had forgotten something. Then, after thinking about it for a few seconds, I turned on my heels and headed back to the carriage. I had to ask just one thing and I thought asking Edward rather than Mr Chambers to be the best course of action. If I could lay this one issue to rest, then everything else that had happened last night could be swept away on a sea of logic also.

"May I ask a question of you, Edward?"

"'Course, Mr Attwood."

"Who found Emily?"

Edward frowned but answered almost immediately. "April, the housemaid. She then alerted Mr and Mrs Chambers."

"Did *you* see her?" I asked. "Where she was found, I mean?"

"No, sir. Not until she was brought downstairs. That was not long before I brought Mr Chambers to see your good self."

I nodded and then leaned in closer, slightly embarrassed by what I was about to ask next and fully expecting Edward to act as if I were a mad man.

"Was there a... a *flower* with her when she was found?"

Edward did not look at me like I was a mad man. He looked at me like I was an imbecile, cocking his head to one side, as if I had just mumbled some alien language.

"I don't know what you mean, Mr Attwood," he said.

"A flower," I told him again. "A lily, in fact. Was there a lily with her?"

Something flickered in the large man's eyes momentarily. I caught it, but it was so quick in passing that I could not register the meaning.

"Why would there be, Mr Attwood?" he then said.

"So, there was not?"

Edward's eyes narrowed and there was definite confusion in the look he gave me this time. No doubt he thought it the strangest question to be asked at this time and by someone as loosely connected to the Chambers family as myself.

So, trying to appear as casual as possible, I merely shrugged, taking his silence as a firm "No", apologised for my rudeness and walked up to the door and rang the bell.

Mr Chambers soon answered and invited me inside. He was dressed in a black suit and looked even smaller than he had the previous day. He was dark under the eyes this morning and his pallor was a sickly off-white. The stress of losing his child had crept up on him overnight and appeared to have aged him by ten years or more.

I asked after his wife and he told me that she was lying down as she felt 'a little off' this morning. I said I understood and told him to offer her my condolences once more. Then I handed him the package.

"I hope you like it," I said and then silently berated myself for such a foolish choice of words.

Like it? An image of his deceased daughter?

Mr Chambers did not seem to notice though and had the photograph open and was studying it with watery eyes barely a second after the words had tumbled from my mouth.

"It is beautiful," he said, smiling through obvious pain. "Perfect."

"I'm glad it meets with your approval, sir," I said, choosing my words more carefully this time.

Mr Chambers handed me some money and I noticed the amount instantly without having to count it. It was double what I had intended to charge.

"This is too much," I said. "Really, I don't-"

"Take it all, Mr Attwood," Chambers interrupted in a polite tone. "Think of the extra as gratitude for the excellent job you have done."

I handed half of the money back to him, which he reluctantly took.

"Thank you," I said, "but I will only take what I deserve. If the photograph had been taken for a happier occasion I would have gladly accepted more as way of appreciation. As it is, I feel terrible for your loss and wish you had never required my services." I tried to fool myself that I had been speaking sincerely, but the truth was that I felt wrong to take the extra money after what had happened during the night. Although all morning I had tried to convince myself that it had all been in my imagination, there was still a small part of me that was not sure and did not want to risk the wrath of an angry spirit child for earning more than necessary from her demise.

Mr Chambers nodded. "I understand, and I respect you for that and so I shall not force the payment on you. However, in return if there is ever anything I can do for you, then please ask."

"Thank you, but I'm sure I'll have no need of a return favour." Out of politeness, I then said, "May I ask how the funeral arrangements are going?"

"Emily's funeral is tomorrow."

"So soon?" I was surprised as I had assumed the period of mourning would be much longer.

"We did not wish to delay it until after Christmas," Chambers said. "Also, there is a risk of heavy snow before the week is out. If we waited then her grave may not be able to be dug and Dr Bernard told us yesterday that her body should not lie in wake for more than a week, in case..."

Mr Chambers did not finish his sentence, as if it were too painful for him. I understood what the family doctor had meant and what Mr Chambers was trying to say. Keeping Emily in the front room, with the fire blazing in the bitter winter, would speed up decay. By the time the funeral came around in the new year, Emily would no longer look like the daughter he once had.

When the solicitor did not speak again there was an uncomfortable silence between us and I was about to bid him good day when I noticed April, the housemaid, through the open door to the kitchen. She looked at me briefly, allowing me to see her young, round face for slightly longer than I had yesterday. I then thought back to Miss Hunter, and her talk of murder.

You found Emily, I thought, watching the housemaid as she busied herself at the sink. *Did* you *think her death was natural? Did* you *think anything suspicious?*

Then, aware that Mr Chambers had much to do and that I should not be concerned with such things, I said that I had better be leaving.

"Of course," he said and opened the front door for me.

"And my thoughts will be with you and your wife tomorrow." With that, I did honestly intend on heading back to Brady when Mr Chambers said something that I had not expected.

"You are welcome to attend, if you wish, Mr Attwood," he said. "It is at one-thirty, at St John's church. People have been asked to meet here at noon."

I did not know what to say, other than I could not say no. I had no appointments tomorrow, and therefore less of an excuse to refuse.

"Thank you," I replied. "I will."

We shook hands again and I left. I passed Edward and doffed my hat to him.

He did the same but the way he looked at me was different than before. His eyes were not as friendly, and he watched me like I was someone who could not be trusted. No doubt my strange question earlier had changed his opinion of me. What he would think of me attending the funeral was anyone's guess, and if he mentioned to Mr Chambers my strange behaviour then even the grieving father might not greet me so warmly tomorrow.

I drove away wondering why I was getting myself more deeply involved in this family's tragedy, and as I thought this, one thing repeated in my mind. For once it was not the sound of a child's cry, but the sound of a child's voice.

"Help me."

13
LAYING WORRIES TO REST

I only had one appointment that afternoon and that was to photograph the store front of a new family bakery that had recently opened. That was booked for two o'clock and so I had some time to kill beforehand. Having skipped breakfast, I stopped for an early lunch at a cafe by the river. After some food and several drinks my mood lightened a little and I was ready for my afternoon's work.

The job went without any problems. The image was simple to capture as the light in the high street was perfect and there was not a hint of a breeze that could cause any blurring of the photograph. The owner, a Mr Henry Fenwick, along with his two sons, posed in front of a window full of loaves and buns, like rulers in front of a new kingdom. Mr Fenwick was more than happy with what I had produced and even paid me a little extra than we had agreed – which I happily accepted this time.

After concluding our business, I was on my way back to Brady who was parked around the corner when a stray breeze (for indeed it was stray, as like I had said, the weather had been very calm) made the sign of the building above me sway and creak loudly, as if wanting me to notice it.

HORACE OLIVER BERNARD
DOCTOR OF MEDICINE
OFFICE HOURS 09.00 – 15.00

This had to be the very same doctor who had dealt with the death of Emily Chambers. I remembered her father had told me that a Dr Bernard had warned them about leaving Emily's body above ground for too long. I had never heard of him before but seeing as this place was only a few streets from where Mr Chambers lived, I doubted that this could be a different person.

(*Help me...*)

I took this as another sign that I could finally put what had been bothering me to rest. According to Edward, there had been no flower left with Emily's body, but could she have really died of something more sinister than a seizure? Could there be a suspicion of murder, as Miss Hunter had spoken of? I doubted it, for if it were murder, surely a medical professional such as this man would have noticed. However, I felt I needed closure in full and I could not waste this opportunity presented to me.

I rang the bell beside the door and, as I waited for an answer, I looked up at the building. It was sandstone yellow and two stories tall. The windows were dark and leaded, and above them the roof was of grey slate which came to a point in the middle, with twin chimney stacks at either end. For a doctor's office, its appearance seemed foreboding and not welcoming in the least, but as a place to live (for I knew that most doctors lived and worked out of the same premises) it was more than a little modest.

A few seconds later, a middle-aged lady half opened the door and poked her head through the gap. She was very plain looking, her skin pale but a healthy clear, and her dark, greying hair was tied back behind her head in a bun. From the little I could see of her body, she appeared to be wearing a white apron over a black blouse and long skirt.

"Can I help you, sir?" she asked, politely.

"I'm here to see Dr Bernard," I said, equally politely and with the added confidence of someone who had a reason for visiting – which I had not.

"You do not have an appointment." It was not a question. She obviously knew I was here unexpectedly.

"No. I'm not even a patient of his," I said, smiling my most charming smile. I still had all my teeth, which even among the wealthy, was a rare sight.

The lady shook her head. "I am very sorry, Mr...?"

"Attwood. Charles Attwood. I'm a photographer." I added my occupation as if it would make a difference.

"I am sorry, Mr Attwood. But I am afraid Dr Bernard is a little busy right now."

"I can wait," I said eagerly. I was not willing to leave so easily. This was my chance to get proof that Emily had died of natural causes and therefore everything last night had been imagined and Miss Hunter's strange behaviour nothing more than female hysteria. "I only need to speak with him for a few minutes. About an important matter. Please?"

She thought on this for a moment and then asked, "Do you wish to register with this practice?"

I shook my head and flashed my most charming smile again. Sometimes, despite my dishevelled look, it worked. "I actually only wish to speak with him regarding a patient off his."

"Oh, I'm afraid that would not be possible," she said sternly. "Dr Bernard cannot divulge patient details."

I widened my smile, showing more of my neat and white front teeth. "I've already been told the patient's medical details. I'm here about my own welfare, but not as a potential patient. May I please come inside and wait?"

The lady looked confused as she hovered behind the half-closed door. Then she eventually said, "The doctor will be finishing for the day soon, but I shall ask him if he will speak to you briefly. But you must promise me, Mr Attwood, that if he cannot help you with what you ask, then you must leave without a scene. This is not only his place of work but his home also."

"Of that I promise, Mrs...?

"*Miss*," she said, correcting me. "*Miss* Grainger."

"...*Miss* Grainger, I promise I'll leave when asked," I said, and meant it. "I'm not here to cause a scene. I simply need to ask one or two questions which the doctor should be able to answer quickly and I'll be gone before you know it."

She looked me over, as if assessing if I was a potential menace or not, so I smiled more and stepped back from the door a little, showing that I meant no harm.

It worked.

"Very well." Miss Grainger opened the door fully and stepped aside to let me in.

"Thank you," I said and removed my hat as I stepped over the threshold.

There was no hallway. Instead, I walked into a reception area that was bright and clean. Cream wallpaper with images of flowers that repeated over and over to form a pattern adorned the walls and there were polished floorboards underfoot. There was desk in one corner of the room which Miss Grainger sat behind before pointing to a row of three chairs beside me and asking me to take a seat. I did so and noticed a door behind the desk which I assumed led into the doctor's private residence and another door off to the left of me which I assumed to be his office as his name was printed on the wood in black ink. From beyond that door, I heard muffled voices, both male.

"Is he in there?" I asked, keeping my voice low.

"Yes. The doctor is with his last patient of the day but should not be too long." With that, Miss Grainger put her head down and began leafing through some papers.

"Are you a nurse?" I asked to make conversation. Since Florence Nightingale had made headline news for her work during the Crimean War a decade earlier, the role of women in the world of medicine had increased in importance, and nursing, as a profession, was on the rise amongst the fairer sex.

Miss Grainger did not look up as she answered me. "More of an assistant really, but I have some medical training. I mainly act as the doctor's secretary and assist clinically only when needed."

That was it. The conversation was over, and so for the next several minutes I sat and planned what I was going to say to Dr Bernard.

As the church-clock along the road tolled three, the door to my left suddenly opened and a gentleman in his late forties showed a younger man out. The older man then looked at me and I bid him good afternoon. He nodded in reply. Then, obviously having no idea who I was or why I was here, he quickly approached Miss Grainger's desk and she whispered something to him. After a few seconds he walked back to me and held out a strong hand.

"I am Dr Horace Bernard," he said. "I believe you wish to speak with me." His voice was strong, the tone deep and powerful. He wore a smart, three-piece suit and was quite tall, his hair thinning on the top but still thick around his ears. His eyes were sharp and inquisitive, and a firm, straight nose sat above a neatly trimmed beard streaked with grey that partially hid a wry smile. All of this gave me the impression that here was a man who was friendly enough on the outside but who would not suffer fools gladly. I had to tread carefully.

I stood and introduced myself as I shook the proffered hand. He then gestured to the office door. "Please, do come inside."

I followed the doctor into the next room. It was a lot smaller than the reception area, with a large oak desk in the centre that dominated most of the space. On one side of it was a cabinet with various bottles and boxes arranged in neat rows and on the other side was an examination table. On the wall behind the desk were several framed certificates from various educational institutions that showed Dr Bernard's credentials that made him superior to the common barber-surgeons of the day. Here was a man of science and learning, a physician who diagnosed illness and disease and treated them using knowledge and medicine rather than with ignorance or religious beliefs.

"And how may I assist you?" he asked as he offered me a seat.

"I'm here regarding the unfortunate death of a Miss Emily Chambers," I said as I sat down opposite him. "I believe you are her family's doctor."

He nodded, solemnly. "Yes, yes, I have been for the last few years, since I inherited this practice from my father. He went off to retire by the seaside and I took over the care of his patients. But yes, Emily was a tragic loss. In some of the poorer areas the death of a child is quite common when you consider that water is dirty, food is short and hygiene is almost unheard of, but for it to happen to such well-to-do people... tragic. But it just goes to show that if the body's time is up, then it is indeed up."

"I agree, it's tragic." I paused, wondering how to go on, but then I became very aware of the doctor waiting for me to continue and so I decided to see where the conversation would lead. "I was wondering if I could speak with you briefly about her condition. A cause of death, you may say. I know you may think me foolish, but I'm worried in case the poor child died of anything contagious."

"I see." Dr Bernard rubbed his beard. I knew he was suspicious of me already. "How did you know the deceased, if I may ask?"

I shrugged. "I didn't really know her. Her father asked me to photograph her body yesterday."

The doctor's eyes suddenly grew wide. He smiled and pointed a finger at me.

"Mr Attwood!" he said aloud and then slapped his thigh. "Yes, I knew I recognised the name. The photographer. I have seen you about, on the bridge, usually when I take my afternoon stroll on a Sunday. Yes, that is how I know of you."

"Yes, that does sound like me," I feigned shyness, hoping it would help my situation when I commenced with the following lie. "Anyway, Mr Chambers told me a cause of death had been determined but didn't disclose the specifics and I didn't wish to ask him to divulge them under the tragic circumstances. But I'll be honest with you, doctor, I'm a weak-minded man, so forgive me, but the reason I am here today is to find out if it's possible for someone to catch an illness from the recently deceased if they'd come into close contact with one."

The doctor frowned and stroked his beard again. Obviously, this man was not easily fooled.

"But I believe that death photography is quite common these days," he said. "I assume that this is not the first time you have performed this service, so why are you all of a sudden concerned by it?"

I thought quickly and replied, "Actually, it *was* my first time, doctor."

He looked surprised. "Really? I have seen you on a weekend. You look quite the expert. Am I not to assume that, unfortunately, you would not be inundated with job offers due to the fad of capturing the dead with the use of a camera?"

"Oh, no, you misunderstand. I've been a photographer for many years. But as for post-mortem photography..." I paused, shook my head, and prepared to lie some more. "Forgive me if I seem above myself but most people who require those services are quite poor, and their hygiene and general health are, for want of a better word, *poor* also. I've always had a fear of sickness and disease and so have always refused to perform such services. But Mr Chambers was a gentleman, and his daughter came from good stock, and so I agreed only this once." I pulled a fake ashamed face. "Also, the money he was offering was too good to turn down."

Bernard smiled, as if he understood. Then he asked, "And you wish to know if you might have contracted something from the deceased girl?"

"That is correct, doctor."

Bernard stared at me a few seconds longer, and then burst out laughing.

"Forgive me finding that amusing," he apologised, "but I have never had anyone ask me that before."

I feigned embarrassment again and said, "Like I explained, I am a weak man, sir."

Just tell me that she died of natural causes, and I'll leave...

"I am very sorry, Mr Attwood," he said, "but I cannot share any personal information with you. I take it you have heard of the Hippocratic Oath we doctors must swear to?"

"I have," I said. "And I know that this is a delicate situation."

"Yes, it is. All I can do is assure you that you were in no danger of contracting any illness from poor Emily Chambers."

That was not enough. I needed a cause of death. I needed closure on this.

"Her father told me that it was some sort of seizure," I said. "I was just wondering if a specific contagious illness may have brought the seizure about?"

Bernard frowned. "I thought Mr Chambers did not divulge the cause of death?"

Yes, this man was very observant. Of course, that was part of his job.

"Oh, did I?" I shook my head. "What I meant was that he told me that much but no more. So, you see, I know what caused Emily to die but not what may have brought it about if you get my meaning."

Bernard sat back in his chair and drummed his fingers on the desk.

"The human body is a very complex machine, Mr Attwood. Because it is so complex it can behave in strange ways from time to time, sometimes very suddenly and without warning. Emily Chambers seemed like a normal, healthy, girl on the outside, but inside something was not right, obviously. My job, as a physician, is to examine the body – eyes, skin, hair, glands, and such like - and ask about her medical history to determine the cause of death. Emily had no history of illness. There was no evidence of external trauma. Her body showed signs of a seizure, which is always the result of a problem starting in the brain rather than the heart or lungs. Simple, sudden and tragic."

"So, her death was due to ill health?" I asked. "Nothing more?"

"Ill health but not illness," he said. "Certainly not contagious."

"Nothing suspicious at all?"

Bernard cocked his head. "Suspicious?"

I quickly corrected myself and said, "So nothing more than natural causes, as a medical person might say. No disease, no accident, no... murder."

Dr Bernard began to look even more confused.

"And how would an accident or a murder be contagious, Mr Attwood?"

I did not answer. Instead, I breathed a fake sigh of relief, quickly stood up and offered him my hand.

"Oh, good," I said, pretending to be flooded with relief as I shook his hand vigorously. "I'm sorry for wasting your time but I'm grateful for you putting my mind at rest. I spent all last night worrying that I may have contracted something deadly. I feel so silly now."

"I am glad to have been of help." The doctor followed me to the door of his office. "Have you always been a nervous fellow,

Mr Attwood? I have some training in the field of mental and nervous health if you ever need to talk."

"Oh, no need for that," I said as we walked back into the waiting room. "You know how some people are. I just need to relax, I suppose."

I thanked the doctor for both his time and hospitality and wished both he and Miss Grainger a merry Christmas. Then I left and headed back to Brady, breathing heavily with relief for real. I may have just made a fool of myself in front of one of the most respected medical professionals within many miles, but it had been worth it. Emily Chambers had died of natural causes. Also, according to Edward, there had been no lily present when her body had been found. These two things formed the simplest of conclusions: Miss Hunter was delusional, and I had imagined everything that had happened last night.

My mind at rest, I headed for home.

It was time to get drunk and have a good night's sleep.

14

STILL UNWILLING TO LISTEN

I arrived home in a jovial mood, looking forward to keeping my appointment with my old friend Burke and sharing a few drinks and laughs. After all, I needed them. I had not relaxed and enjoyed myself much since I had returned from America and my experiences there had left me on the verge of a broken man. I now felt it was time to finally let go of the past and look ahead to the future, but, when I steered Brady and the cart into my gloomy yard, all thoughts of a bright future evaporated like steam from a boiling pot when I saw the figure by the back door to my house. It moved towards me purposefully as I halted my horse and a little light that spilled down from a nearby streetlamp illuminated the soft, attractive features of the person soon stood in front of me.

I sighed. I did not need this right now.

"Hello, Miss Hunter," I said as I climbed down from the cart. "I'll not ask how you know where I live as it's quite clear you read my address on the side of the darkroom yesterday. I will ask, however, what it is that you want, and if it's not to hire my services then I'd appreciate it if you'd leave."

Miss Hunter ignored me and instead turned her attention to Brady. She stroked his nose and the horse seemed to enjoy it, snorting with pleasure whilst moving closer for more.

"I knocked at the front door but received no answer," she said. "So, I came around the back and saw that your cart was missing. It was coming in dark and so I knew that you would be back soon and so I waited. I hope you do not mind."

"I do," I said, but she ignored me again and instead told Brady how wonderful he was. The horse seemed to like it, and appeared to instantly take to Miss Hunter, and that, for some reason, annoyed me even more. "What do you want?"

"I went to see Mr Chambers again this morning," she said. "To see if he would listen to me after what had happened to his daughter. He told me to leave and said that if

I bothered him anymore then he would have me arrested."

I began unloading my equipment from my darkroom, placing them piece by piece on the ground next to my feet as I told her, "I don't blame him. After all, he has just lost his daughter. The last thing he needs is for you to pile more misery on him with talk of murder."

Miss Hunter stopped patting Brady and turned to me.

"Just let me tell you what I know, Mr Attwood."

I stopped unloading my equipment and threw up my hands in despair. "Why me?"

"Because I have no one else to turn to," she said. "Mr Chambers does not want to help because he does not want to admit the truth."

"The truth about what? Emily being murdered and the culprit leaving flowers behind?" I said it as if I thought it to be ridiculous, but somewhere deep inside, I shivered at the thought of it still being true.

"Yes," she said, unfazed. "I know who killed Emily, *and* my nephew."

"Your nephew?"

"Yes, my nephew, Adam, was also a victim and had a lily left with his body. He died because of what his father had done, and I fear Emily has suffered the same fate for what *her* father has done."

"I haven't got time for this," I told her. Even though I was more than a little intrigued to hear what she might have to say, I stayed resolute with my decision not to have any further involvement with this situation. "I'm afraid I have an appointment to keep."

I unlocked the back door and took my camera inside the house. When I came back out for the rest of my equipment Miss Hunter was still there. I sighed again and said, "Look, I don't mean to be rude, but I think you're mistaken about all of this. Mr Chambers said that his daughter died of natural causes. I also confirmed that with her doctor today."

"Why did you speak with the doctor?" she asked. "Did you not believe Mr Chambers?"

I went to see him because you had gotten inside my head, I thought, but I said, "If you're so concerned about this then why don't you go to the police?"

She shrugged. "You do not believe me. Why would they?"

"Because that's their job. They're meant to investigate these things, not me."

She gave a small, sharp laugh. "I am a woman, Mr Attwood, so I already have little credibility when it comes to issues such as this, and they will think me insane if I tell them that a ghost is responsible."

Normally I would have laughed at such nonsense, but after last night I was less inclined to.

(*Help me...*)

"A ghost?" I said, trying my best to sound amused. I picked up the rest of my equipment, feeling more pity than anger towards this poor wreck of a woman. "Please leave, Miss Hunter."

I went inside and placed my things in my study. When I came back out, I locked the door and un-hitched Brady from the cart. Miss Hunter was standing next to me as I did so, but I acted as if she were not there at all.

"I have evidence of what I say," she said as I began to lead Brady out of the yard. "I can show you. Please, Mr Attwood..."

"Goodnight, Miss Hunter," I said as I headed out onto the street.

Fully expecting her to follow and harass me some more, I looked back over my shoulder in time to see her leave my yard and walk off in the opposite direction. Hopefully she had finally realised that I had no time for her outrageous claims and bother me no more.

Relieved slightly, I saw Brady to the stables and headed straight for the pub.

I needed a drink.

15
OLD FRIENDS, NEW WORRIES

I entered the Iron Horse at a quarter to five. It was full and rowdy, the sound of raised voices and drunken laughter echoing about the place and the potential for trouble always imminent. Tobacco smoke hung in the air like a noxious cloud and the smell of spilled beer mingled with the odour of dirty breath and unwashed bodies. Behind it all, was the aroma of hot food and, seeing as I had some time before Burke would arrive, I ordered something hot and filling.

    I ate at my usual table, holding a chair opposite me for Burke. At one point, just as I finished my meal and the bartender took away my plate, a lady of the night sat opposite me, calling me 'Darling'. She was about forty, with a plump face, ragged hair and wearing tattered old clothes that stank of damp and mould. She had a sore on her top lip and her left eye was bruised. She had no teeth in some places and black or yellowing ones in the others. I told her the seat was taken and she said she could show me a good time. I told her I was not interested in a good time and so she called me a 'queer' and moved onto the next table where a scruffy man twice her size sat her on his lap. They left together a couple of minutes later, no doubt to find somewhere dark and secluded to conclude their business. Just as they walked out the pub, Burke arrived. He sat down opposite me and called over to the barman for two ales.

"You just missed an arrest," I told him in fun. "A prostitute and a client."

"Who?" he asked, looking around behind him.

"The two who just left as you came in."

He raised an eyebrow and as the bartender brought our drinks he said, "Oh well, never mind, my shift finished half an hour ago anyway."

He paid for the drinks and tapped his tankard against mine before downing half his ale in one go.

"So," he then said, wiping froth from his top lip as he looked about the room, "this is where you hang out, is it? Very nice."

"Hey, enough talk like that," I said, jokingly, "you think you're too good to drink in a place like this since you got promoted?"

He smiled, proudly. "You heard about that?"

"I read it in the paper yesterday. Whose boots did you have to kiss to become an inspector?"

Burke laughed and called over to the barmen for two more beers. "No boot kissing, just hard work, my friend. Hard work."

I knew he was speaking the truth. Despite the drawback of being born into a poor family, Burke had sought out a decent education whilst working several jobs to help support his parents and now, at the age of thirty-eight, he was reaping the rewards with a well-paid career and a loving family.

"Speaking of work," he then said, "you seem to being doing alright judging by what I saw one the bridge yesterday."

"Yes," I said. "Business is good."

The barman brought our drinks and I paid for them. Burke then said, "Tell me about America."

So, I reluctantly did. I told him about my four-week sail over there on a ship called the *Joanna* and my journey to Washington to speak with government and army officials. I explained about the parts of the country that were safe to travel to and those that were not so safe. I told him about some of the places I had photographed and some of the people who posed for me. He asked if I had witnessed any battles and I told him I had not, that because I was a civilian, I had to remain several miles behind any regiment when journeying to any potentially dangerous areas. I did tell the truth and say that I had come across several battle sites a few days after the fighting was over and did see many bodies and even more injured and traumatised soldiers. I talked about the hardships I faced out there, the days when I was hot and thirsty, and the nights when I was cold and hungry and the time I fell ill with a fever and naturally thought I would die in agony in the middle of nowhere.

I did not tell him about the Indian reservation I came across.

I did not tell him about the crying I heard on the wind.

Finally, I told him that I had returned to England because I had done what I had set out there to do and had no reason to stay any longer.

When I finished, Burke asked, "When's the big exhibition?"

"Oh, not for some time yet," I said, lying. "When I get around to it."

"So, in the meantime you make your money doing street photography?"

"Not only that," I said. "I do other things. I photographed a bakers shop today."

"Wow," Burke said, sarcastically. "Hardly photographing the queen or prime minister is it? You're a talented man, Charlie. You should be putting your skills to good use."

"Thanks for the advice."

"Anytime, my friend."

"Well," I then said, "that's all that's been happening with me. It's your turn now. What's been going on in the world of crime and punishment since I've been away?"

Burke shrugged. "Oh, you know, there's always something going on; robberies, assaults – fortunately nothing more than that at the minute."

"I read about the murder case you solved recently."

Burke took a swig of his drink and nodded.

"Strange case, that one," he then said.

"I'm intrigued. Tell me."

"Where to start...?" He pulled out his tobacco and prepared a pipe. I did the same. "The victim was called Jeffery Parsons. He was in his seventies. A retired teacher - well, sort of. He used to teach Sunday school in a place called St Simon's Hall, over on Medway street. It used to be one of those places where kids who worked during the week could get an education on their one day off."

"Like you used to?"

"Exactly," Burke lit his pipe and sucked back several hits of tobacco. "Anyway, it closed down years ago and had remained empty. Parsons' house backed onto the hall, and he lived there alone as his wife was long dead. His neighbours said he was a quiet man who kept himself to himself. Had no enemies, that sort of thing."

I puffed on my pipe and said, "Well, he obviously had one. He was murdered, right?"

Burke nodded. "About a month ago, one of the neighbours reported to the police that she had seen someone inside the old hall at night, probably a drunk or a vagrant. They had tried alerting Mr Parson's but never received an answer after knocking at his door. The police went to the hall and found a homeless man, this Arthur Olsen character, who had been staying there the past few nights. Mr Parsons still owned the building and when the police went to his house to tell him about the vagrant on his property, they too got no answer. The neighbour then said that he had not seen Mr Parsons for several days and so, out of concern for his welfare, the police broke down the door and found his body. That's when I was called in."

"I take it the police knew it was murder from the start and suspected this Olsen fellow?"

"Yes, but it wasn't that simple. Let's put it this way; both the front and back doors were locked from inside, and so were all the windows. Mr Parsons was found tied to his bed with a copper pipe forced down his throat, and I mean *forced*. Most of his teeth had been broken in the process. There were several empty jars and bottles of household chemicals and poisons by the bed. Someone had poured the lot into this pipe and down his throat until his insides burned and bled and he choked to death in agony. Of course, we suspected Olsen and took him into custody, but we couldn't charge him until we could prove he had gotten into the house somehow. How he got in was a mystery - a real locked room mystery. We knew he had to have gotten in somehow. He couldn't walk through walls. He wasn't a ghost." Burke laughed and I joined in, despite my unease at the mention of such things.

"Anyway, I searched the hall and I found that behind the main classroom, there was a smaller room, like an office or a study. In the wall that it shared with the house, we found a hidden panel. It looked just like a regular wall panel, but we found it was hinged and could be opened outward. A secret passage led through the wall to a similar hidden panel in Mr Parson's kitchen. I don't know what it was for, maybe a quick way to get from the house to the school if he was running late. You know what some of these old buildings are like with their little cubby holes and things. Anyway, what it was for was irrelevant. We had the means of which Olsen had entered the house and committed the crime and he was prosecuted for it."

"He admitted it?" I asked. "Once you found the hidden passage?"

"Oh, no," Burke said. "He denied it more, claiming he had no knowledge of it. But he was the murderer. He was the only one who could have done it."

I thought about this and then asked, "So why did he do it?"

Burke shrugged and said, "Why does anyone do anything? He was hungry. Maybe he found the hidden passage by accident and went into the house to find food? Maybe Mr Parsons caught him, and Olsen attacked him."

"And tied him to the bed and force fed him poison? Why not just strangle the old man or something?"

Burke shrugged. "Charlie-boy, I've been a detective for ten years and a lot of the stuff I could tell you wouldn't make sense. People are a funny lot, and sometimes act in strange ways."

"That *is* strange," I said, sipping my drink and wondering what would cause someone to act that way.

"It certainly is," Burke said. Then, quietly, almost to himself, he added, "So was the flower."

My heart dropped into my boots.

The pub seemed to fall silent.

Time seemed to stop.

"Flower?" I asked.

"Yes," Burke said. "We kept it out of the press release because it didn't seem that important, just weird. Olsen left a flower on Mr Parsons's body. Placed it on his chest, as if it were a sign of remorse or guilt or something. Maybe he thought that by leaving a token like that he would be forgiven for killing the old man."

I barely heard a word of what Burke had just said. I did not care why he thought the flower had been left there. I just needed to know what type of flower it had been, and so I asked.

Burke frowned, obviously wondering why out of all the questions to ask I had asked that one.

"What type of flower?" He shrugged, like it meant nothing. "A lily. A single, white lily."

16
EMILY RETURNS

I did not mention to Burke that Miss Hunter had told me that a lily had also been left with her nephew's body. I also knew why I did not tell him. It was because I was scared to admit that Miss Hunter may have been telling the truth this whole time, therefore making it possible that Emily Chambers had also been murdered and had indeed haunted me the previous night. So, I left it alone and the subject soon changed, and Burke and I spent the rest of our time mostly chatting about everything and nothing - though it was hard for me to relax and enjoy myself after what I had heard. Soon the time tolled nine and he said he had to leave to get back to his family. I said I would stay and finish my drink and he told me that we should catch up again soon. He knew my address and where to find me on a Sunday, so he would be in touch. Then he waved and left the pub, drunk and merry.

    I finished my drink and then ordered another. Then I bought a bottle of gin to take with me and I was back home by half-past the hour and both the downstairs and upstairs fires were lit fifteen minutes later. Then, retiring to bed, alone with my thoughts, my mind dwelt on Jeffery Parsons' murder and the lily that had been left with his body. Burke had said the flower had not been mentioned in the newspaper report, so Miss Hunter could not have known about it unless what she had told me about her nephew was true. But what connected her nephew and the murder of Jeffery Parsons to the death of Emily Chambers?

I knew I was in for a restless night. For once it was not the thought of my impending nightmare which made me uncomfortable. Instead, because I was very much aware that my mind was stressed and my imagination may run wild, I might have another experience like that of the previous night. However, twenty minutes later, and with half the gin drank (on top of the several ales I had already consumed), instead of being tense and nervous at the thought of another nocturnal visit from a little, dead girl, I felt giddy and relaxed. The alcohol had dulled my senses to the point where the world and my worries seemed amusing rather than troublesome. In fact, I was so drunk, I even began to taunt the ghost I did not want to believe in.

"Hey, Emily," I called. "Let me see you. If you want me to help, then show yourself."

I laughed aloud drunkenly and stared deep into the darkness of my room, the only light the burning red coals on the fire.

"Ha! Come on, Emily, show yourself, and bring that flower with you." I swigged from the bottle and waited, hoping that nothing would happen. "Nonsense!" I cried. "It's humbug, as Mr Scrooge would say!"

Soon my eyes felt gritty, as though sand had been poured onto them, and I yawned deeply, my body craving rest.

By eleven, with three-quarters of the gin gone, I placed the bottle on the floor, lay back and let unconsciousness embrace me like a long-lost friend.

*

Like the previous night, several hours passed before it happened.

*

I do not think a noise woke me this time - at least I cannot remember any such sound. I simply opened my eyes and sat up in bed, as if propelled by some unseen force. I knew immediately that I was not yet done sleeping as my eyes stung, my vision was blurred, and my head was woozy with the effects of alcohol that still lingered within my system. Yet, for some reason, I knew that something was not quite right and that I had been roused from sleep by something other than my own actions, and so I ignored the impulse to lie back down. Instead, I sat rigid, my eyes wide and owl-like, my ears pricked like those of small prey that have heard a predator. I listened and looked, and as I did so I felt a now familiar rising panic inside of me. My heart began to beat faster. A slick sweat broke out on my forehead. The hairs on my arms stood up and the skin beneath them chilled.

Then I heard it, and my heart stopped racing and instead seemed to cease beating altogether.

The noise came from downstairs. It had been the same dull shuffle and thud I had heard last night, only this time it had seemed louder and not as muffled.

Instantly, I knew why.

Last night the noise had come from the study and so an extra door had blocked most of the sound. This time, however, it seemed to come from the foot of the stairs.

Suddenly I remembered calling out for Emily earlier, mocking her, assuming her ghost to be nonsense, but now I felt quite differently. I sat still for eternal seconds, telling myself that I was again imagining things and promising myself that starting tomorrow I would cut back on drinking, eventually stopping altogether as it was obviously rotting my brain. Besides, even if last night Emily had magically escaped the photograph and dragged her corpse about my study, she could not do so tonight. The photograph was no longer in my possession.

It was in her own home. Let her haunt her parents and beg them for help!

Then I heard it again - another drag, and another thud - but before the noise had a chance to send shivers of fear through me, my eyes were drawn to something far more terrifying.

A single lily, its stem green and fresh, its petals white and healthy, its scent strong and musky, lay on top of the blanket at the foot of my bed, as if it had been placed there with love.

Instinctively, I swept it away as if it were a poisonous snake, and it seemed to disappear into the darkness of my room, floating in the air for a second before vanishing in front of my very eyes.

Before I had time to comprehend what had just happened, the noise from downstairs came again and that seemed to summon up any courage left in me.

I reached down by the bed for the iron bar, and as I did so I felt that sinking feeling one gets when they realise something is amiss. You see, I had forgotten to bring it back up to my room after venturing downstairs with it the previous night. I was without defence!

Against what? A ghost? The restless spirit of a young girl?

Whatever *was* down there, I had to do something to protect myself, so I picked up the bottle of gin (drinking some first, obviously, before corking it again) and climbed out of bed. As I did, I noticed the time on my pocket watch on the bedside table.

It was three minutes past three in the morning.

I turned the bottle over in my hand and held the neck-end so that the body of the bottle could be used like a club as I slowly, shakily, edged my way towards the partially open bedroom door. I could not see much of the staircase from where I was and nothing at all of downstairs. What little flickering illumination the dying fire cast merely made my surroundings go from black to grey and then back to black. For the first few steps I heard nothing more, and relief began to trickle through my body, warming me more than any fire ever could. Halfway to the door, I was ready to consign myself to the fact that I had again imagined something that was not real until another noise stopped me dead.

The sound was a dull, echoing thud followed by silence for a couple of seconds. Then it came again. And again. Growing louder. Getting closer. And then I realised that whatever was making it was coming up the staircase.

I began to tremble. The liquid inside the bottle I carried began to jostle and jump, like waves on a tormented sea. My hand then must have tightened around the neck without my knowledge and the cork popped, spilling the contents down my leg and onto the floor. But that was the least of my worries.

Thud!
Pause.
Thud!
Pause.

It is her! Emily! Crawling up the stairs, still attached to my apparatus! That noise is the base block she is dragging with her, thudding against the steps as she somehow makes her way up to get me!

I swallowed hard and forced my leaden legs to move. My best chance was to reach the door and close it fully. There was a cabinet nearby that I could pull in front of it as a barricade.

But surely a ghost can pass through a door?

A ghost can go wherever it wants to!

I shuffled forwards and looked through the gap to the staircase outside as the thudding continued. Then, suddenly, down there in the dark, I saw something small and pale swiftly break free from the shadows and clutch at one of the steps not far from the top of the flight. It was a child's hand, and I cannot begin to describe the terror that filled me right then, nor do I believe I ever will.

I backed away from the door so that I could no longer see outside the bedroom as the terrible thudding continued, the thing that was once Emily Chambers slowly dragging her dead body to the top of the stairs until finally coming to a stop on the small landing outside my room. I caught the scent of sweet perfume along with that hideous shuffling, dragging sound as she now approached my bedroom door.

"Em... Emily?" I stammered.

Almost immediately, in the gap between the door and its frame, a blank, pale face shrouded by long, dark hair suddenly jerked into view.

I dropped the bottle as shock caused my hand to flex open and it shattered on the floorboards by my feet. Somehow, without thinking, I raced forward and managed to slam the door shut on the thing lurking outside my bedroom. I then quickly hurried to the cabinet and put all my strength behind it, pushing it in front of the door, its base grinding and squealing as it scraped across the floorboards.

As I backed away, my night-clothes sticking to me with perspiration, the door handle suddenly began to rattle and shake. Then came the very worst part...

"Help me..."

The voice, though obviously that of a girl, was also not of this earth. Somehow, it was both soft and feminine yet guttural and hoarse.

"Help me, please..."

I jumped into my bed and pulled the blanket up to my chin as the twisting and pulling on the door handle become more violent and desperate.

"Help me," the voice from the other side of the door said, again and again, and each time the words grew louder and more desperate, and more guttural and animalistic until I could take no more.

"HELP ME!"

I pulled my pillow over my head and squeezed tight to block out her voice as the rattling of the door against the frame became so violent that I was certain it would explode inwards and sweep aside the heavy cabinet as if it were made of nothing but feathers.

"PLEASE, HELP MEEEEEEEE!!!"

17
STARTING TO BELIEVE

My horse is still rearing up with fear and I am certain that he will bolt at any second and leave me here alone, stranded in this Hellish place.

But I do not turn back. Not yet.

The woman's body is only a few yards away and the crying – the screaming – is still howling about the camp.

I then notice the buffalo-hide blanket beside the woman's body, one of her arms still over it, protectively. When she had fallen, when the bullet or bayonet that had taken her life and caused her to fall where she lay, she had been clutching something precious, something so precious that even as she took her final breath she had refused to let go.

I notice the blanket move and I tell myself it is the wind disturbing it. But deep down, no matter how hard I try to convince myself otherwise, I know the wind has nothing to do with what I see or indeed hear.

It's a child! *I think.* A crying infant!

I wonder what to do. I am alone in a strange place with little food and water, and I am recovering from a fever. I do not know if I can look after myself let alone something so young and weak.

The blanket moves once more and that is when I make a decision that will haunt me in my sleep for the rest of my life.

I quickly turn and hurry back to my horse.

As I ride off, the wind cuts through me, sending tears spilling from my eyes and down my cheeks, and with it, always, is the sound of the crying child I leave behind...

I awoke with a start and knew it was morning as the nightmare (which always occurred right at the end of my night's sleep to be fresh in my brain upon waking) had played out to its grim conclusion.

I still felt the effects of the terror I had experienced during the night. My body felt stiff and aching, and my hands trembled as I sat up in bed and looked around my room.

The fire was dead in the grate. The door was locked. The only obvious signs that something had occurred was the cabinet in front of the door and the smashed bottle of gin in the centre of the room, the contents having since soaked into the floorboards.

I climbed out of bed and rubbed my face hard to warm up my senses before pulling the cabinet back to its original place and stepping out onto the landing.

As I looked down the stairs, the front door opened and Miss Dawson entered, carrying in my fresh clothes. I assumed it to be around the hour of nine, and despite only being dressed in my long underclothes, I hurried down the stairs towards the cleaning lady. I needed some company. I needed someone to talk to.

Just like Miss Hunter wanted to talk to you...?

"Mornin', Mr Attwood," Miss Dawson said before quickly averting her eyes upon seeing what I was wearing. "Sorry, I didn't know you weren't decent again. That's two days in a row, now. But at least I'm on time today. Nine on the dot."

I greeted her as warmly as I could before apologising for my appearance. I also added that I had not slept well the previous night.

"Oh, I'm sorry to hear that," she said. "Workin' late again?"

I said I had not been.

"Hope you weren't ill."

"No," I said.

"Bad dreams?" She laughed. I did not.

"Do you believe in ghosts, Miss Dawson?" I asked.

She frowned and said, "Ghosts, Mr Attwood? As in spirits that have not moved on?"

"Exactly," I said. "That is *exactly* what I mean."

"Why do you ask?"

"I think I've seen one," I said. "A young girl. Here, in my home. Last night."

"A ghost of a girl?" Miss Dawson neither looked shocked nor surprised. Merely curious. "A girl you know?"

"Sort of. Do you believe me?"

She looked at me, at the wreck I must have appeared at that moment and said, "I believe you must have seen somethin', Mr Attwood, you look quite a state, if you don't mind me sayin' so. What did this ghost girl want?"

"Help," I said. "She said she wanted help."

"And why would she be in need of help? Help in movin' on to the spirit world?"

I shook my head. I thought back to my conversation with Burke about the Jeffery Parsons murder case, and to Miss Hunter, and the way she was convinced Emily had been murdered also, just like her nephew.

"No," I said. "I think she wants me to help catch the person responsible for her death?"

Miss Dawson gasped. "She was murdered? How?"

"I don't know yet." I realised that I had said the word 'yet', as if at some point in the near-future I would find the answer. "Do you believe me? Do you think it's possible that this could happen?"

"You look tired, Mr Attwood," Miss Dawson said, looking at me with what I took as a mixture of pity and a little fear. "Are you sure you're not just in need of more sleep?"

"I saw her!" I sat down on the bottom stair and put my head in my hands.

"Should I fetch a doctor, Mr Attwood?"

I looked up through the gaps in my fingers. "You don't believe me, do you?"

"Ghosts?" The cleaning lady appeared to think about it for a few seconds. Then she said, "I'm not sure, Mr Attwood. There're a lot of these mediums about these days that say ghosts and spirits are very real, but I can't help think it funny that if they do exist that they waited until so recently to make an appearance."

I sighed, although I was unsure why. In a way, I wanted her to say that the notion of spectres and spirits was nonsense, but I also wanted her to say that such things could very much be real. Either way, something was wrong. I was either going insane or being haunted.

"So, you don't believe in things like that?" I asked her. "That when people die that their spirits may linger, especially if they're taken before their natural time?"

Miss Dawson shrugged. "If that were the case then we wouldn't be able to move for ghosts, would we? Think of all the deaths throughout history. There must be thousands of spirits wanderin' about."

"But what if only some spirits don't move on?" I said, trying to convince her. "What if certain ones cannot? What if some *refuse* to move on for some reason?"

Miss Dawson placed my clothes on the floor and then put her hands on her hips. She looked at me like someone would a child that has awoken from a bad dream and needed reassuring. Indeed, I believe right then that I may have taken on a childlike demeaner as I sat on the bottom stair with my legs tucked up to my chest.

"I think there's more to life than what we know," she then said. "As for what you just asked, about spirits not movin' on, it's possible I suppose, but maybe there's somethin' else at work when people experience what they assume to be a hauntin'."

I nodded, eager to hear more, to hear *anything* that could help explain what I had witnessed. "Such as?"

Miss Dawson sat down beside me. Her leg accidentally brushed mine and it felt good to be close to someone. It felt comforting and real.

"I have a story that might help explain what I mean," she said, looking off into the distance, as if trying to recall a past memory. "When I was young, when my father was alive, he told me somethin'. It was Christmas Eve night when I was six or seven and in keepin' with tradition, I asked him to tell me a ghost story. So, to my surprise, instead of inventing one, he told me about somethin' that had happened to him one time at work. He worked in the East docks, you see, unloadin' the cargo and stuff. Anyway, he told me that when he was younger, before I was born, he worked alongside his best friend, a man named Callum Abbott. They'd known each other all their lives and were as close as brothers and trusted each other more than anyone else they knew – which was good, as the job they did was not without its dangers and so workin' with someone you knew would look out for your safety made it a little easier. Strong winds could often blow a man off the docks and into the freezin' water below, or a person may be crushed when a load broke away from the chains holdin' it. They were the only two dangers he told me about, Mr Attwood, and only those, because those are the only two that matter in this story. The most important thing to remember is that my father knew of the dangers each time he went to work. He knew he may be hurt or worse, and it was always in the front of his mind, like he was expectin' it to happen someday."

I nodded but wondered where she was going with this.

"One night, whilst they were at work one winter, my father took ill and had to leave early as he could not catch his breath for this terrible flu that had infected his lungs. Later, that same night, Callum was blown into the sea and, despite being a confident swimmer, was drowned by a strong current. Had my father been there, he said, he would have seen his friend and may have been able to arrange for a rescue of Callum within seconds. However, as it was, no one noticed that Callum was missing until it was too late. My father was devastated upon learning the news and he said it set back his recovery by another two weeks. In a way, he always blamed himself, although no one will ever know if it would have made a difference had he been there." Miss Dawson looked at me, as if she knew I had no idea why she was telling me this, but that I would soon enough. "Anyway, a few weeks later, my father was back at work, although he said it never felt the same without Callum by his side. This one particular night, a ship was lowerin' a crate of fruit that had come over from Africa and my father and a new worker, a young lad called Tom Underwood, were waitin' below to help unhook the chains when my father suddenly heard someone call for help. He said the voice sounded as if someone was in the water, so he quickly headed over to the side of the dock and shone his lamp but could see nothin' but the churnin' water below. But he could still hear the shouts for help. What was more, is that he was certain the voice he heard was that of his friend, Callum Abbott. My father then called for his workmate to come over, and this Mr Underwood did so, and joined my father away from their positions, looking down into the water. My father asked him if he could hear shoutin' and the other man replied that he couldn't, yet, to my father's ears at least, the shoutin', the *beggin'* for help, was very real and so he remained where he was, holdin' his lamp over the side of the dock to illuminate the freezin' water twenty feet below, searchin' for the man." Miss Dawson paused for effect and looked me in the eye. "That's when it happened, Mr Attwood. That's when the crate that would have been above my father - had he been where he should have - snapped from its chains and dropped to the ground, shatterin' its contents everywhere and sure to have crushed anyone standin' beneath it."

My eyes widened upon hearing this and I thought I had understood the point of this strange tale. "The ghost of his friend saved your father?"

Miss Dawson shrugged and said, "Some people may say so. However, my father, right up until his death, swore somethin' else entirely. He thought it was merely his mind playin' tricks on him. Like he said to me back then, if it was Callum's ghost coming to save him then why was it shoutin' for help? Why didn't Callum just appear and warn my father about the accident about to happen?"

I was a little perplexed by this. "So, your father thought the accident was just a coincidence?"

"Maybe it was." Miss Dawson stood up and walked back to the pile of my clothes she had brought in with her. "But my father said one more thing that I think may help you understand. He didn't believe in ghosts, nor was he a particularly clever man, but he knew that there were things on earth that most of us will never understand no matter how hard we try. He thought that maybe somehow, somewhere deep inside, he knew that the accident was about to happen that night and so his mind created an illusion – an excuse – to take himself out of harms way."

I stood up, confused even more now. "What are you saying, Miss Dawson? What has that got to do with ghosts?"

She smiled. "Maybe nothin', maybe everythin'. Maybe, just maybe, that people who think they see ghosts are actually seein' somethin' that their mind has created. Maybe the ghost is not the spirit of someone who's returned because *they* are in need of help, but maybe the person who *sees* the ghost is the one in need of help." She picked up my clothes and smiled, thinly. "I'll hang these up, change your bedding and be on my way, Mr Attwood."

With that she headed up the stairs, leaving me to think about what she had told me.

But I could not think for long, for I had a funeral to attend.

18
A MORBID GATHERING

Miss Dawson finished her chores and I thanked her, paid her double her fee and wished her a Merry Christmas. She asked if I was alright after our little chat earlier and I lied and said I was. The truth was that I was certain of what had happened last night (I could deny these things no more) and after listening to my cleaning lady's tale I was even more sure that someone needed help, be that either Emily or myself. However, I told Miss Dawson that I had not long woken before she arrived and a dream must have lingered in my mind, causing me to act strangely. I asked her to forget what I had said about ghosts and such-like and that I felt quite silly now having woken up more. She said that she would not dream of saying a word to anyone (which I knew was impossible for her) and bid me good day and said she would see me next week. I saw her out and waved her off before I quickly washed and shaved and changed into my black suit. Then I thought about how I was going to get to the Chambers' residence.

I did not feel like taking my own horse and so decided to hail a hansom cab. Once outside in the fresh morning air, though, and realising that I had over an hour still to spare, I decided to walk and take an extended route along the Thames before heading West at the Abbey. This also gave me thinking time. I had to do something about this Emily situation. I had to talk to someone other than Miss Dawson. If only I knew how to get in contact with Miss Hunter. Perhaps Mr Chambers knew her address? But, I thought, could I really ask him about her today of all days? Then I thought, what about my friend inspector Burke? He could help me find Miss Hunter's address! But did I want to involve my only friend in all of this and have him think me crazy too? I was at a loss and time flew by as it tends to do when you are not looking forward to something, and before I knew it, noon was not far off, and I was still no closer on deciding what to do or with whom to speak with about my problems.

I arrived at the Chambers' house at the same time as several other mourners. I did not speak to any of them (nor them to me) as I entered, the atmosphere inside heavy and depressing, as if the sorrow everyone felt had merged into an unseen entity capable of sucking all happiness and colour from the surrounding environment. The hallway seemed darker than on my previous visits and the walls closer. The ceiling seemed lower and threatening, and I craved a drink of something strong as claustrophobia began to settle into my bones. I then realised that for the first time in weeks I had not started my day with several gulps of gin and suddenly I did not feel well at all. I started to sweat. I started to shake. I considered leaving and going straight to the nearest public house to drown my sorrows. Then I saw Mr Chambers at the door to the living room, shaking hands with those that were in front of me and I realised that my problems paled in comparison to those of certain others.

I removed my hat and held out an unsteady hand when it was my turn to enter.

"Glad you could come, Mr Attwood," he said, and I thought it an odd thing to say but assumed it was apt.

I gave a small, pitiful smile but did not say anything in reply. Then, glad that there were people behind me, I entered the living room, leaving the pained father to greet the other mourners.

There was at least twenty people in the living room. In the centre, in her open coffin, lay Emily, although from where I was stood, I could not see much of her for the many family members and friends gathered around, paying their last respects. April, the housemaid, was dressed in a smart black dress and was offering glasses of sherry from a tray. I took one and thanked her, but she never acknowledged the gratitude. In fact, she looked like her mind was somewhere else, like all of this was a bad dream she may hopefully soon wake up from.

You found her, I thought. *You know the truth. You know that Emily did not die of a seizure...*

I suddenly felt the urge to ask the maid what she had seen when she entered Emily's room that fateful morning, but she moved away to hand out more drinks before I could. I decided that had been the best thing as asking such questions would not have been ideal right now. The poor young woman was obviously still traumatised from making the macabre discovery and she did not need reminding of it.

I sipped my drink (for once not enjoying the tang of alcohol early in the day) as more and more people entered the room. It suddenly felt very crowded and as I searched for space to stand by myself, I noticed Dr Bernard talking to three men over by the piano. I raised my glass to greet him, and he did the same, however I felt by his facial expression that he wondered, quite rightly, why I was even here. The family doctor was expected. A photographer was not. I then spotted Mrs Chambers with a group of people over the far side of the room, and she made her way over to me almost immediately.

"Mr Attwood, thank you for coming," she said. Her voice had more confidence to it than when I had last spoken to her, as if the finality of the situation had sculpted a rock of courage within her. Either that, or maybe she was simply all cried out.

"I just wanted to pay my respects," I said. "Again, my condolences."

Mrs Chambers pointed to the wall and my eyes followed the trail of her finger to the picture I had taken just two days before. It had been placed above the hearth and two bouquets of flowers had been placed either side of it.

"People have commented on it," she said. "They are amazed at your skill. Thank you again for such a grand job."

I took the compliment with humility. "Like I said the other day, those are the jobs I wish I never had to do. No amount of money is worth the pain and suffering of others."

Mrs Chambers dabbed at her eyes with a handkerchief, and I took it that it was a gesture rather than out of need. "Yes. Time will make it easier we hope, but right now the pain is still very fresh." She looked over at the coffin that was still hidden by a group of mourners. Then, almost to herself, she said, "You never think it will happen to you. Do you have children, Mr Attwood?"

"I do not," I replied.

She smiled, and it was bittersweet. "They are the most precious things in the world. You will do anything for them, and in an instant they can be taken from you. Life can be so, so cruel." She then noticed more people arriving and excused herself to go and greet them.

Not knowing what else to do, I followed the queue of mourners in front of me towards the open coffin and soon found myself looking down upon Emily's body.

I cannot truly describe the depressing sensation I felt in the pit of my stomach when I saw her.

Her skin had paled more, and her cheeks had sunken in, giving her face the appearance of drastic weight loss. She was still wearing the dress from two days earlier and her hair was styled the same way, yet it looked limp and fragile. Her clothes had been sprayed with more perfume and the smell more than anything reminded me of her visitations the last two nights.

(*"Help me..."*)

I can't help you, I thought.

(*"Please, help me..."*)

I don't know how...

"You take a fine picture," a voice behind me suddenly said.

I spun round. It was Edward. The big man, obviously having been given the day off to mourn along with the family, was dressed in black and held a drink in one of his giant hands.

"Good to see you again." I shook his hand.

Edward then motioned to the photograph with his drink. "You have talent, Mr Attwood. Anyone would swear that picture was taken when poor Emily were still alive."

We then both looked down at the coffin again. At what remained of a young life that had ended too soon.

"Thank you," I replied. "I only wish it had been."

Then, sensing that others behind us were wishing to pay their respects also, we both moved to a space by the bay window at the front of the room. I did not know what to say to Edward to start a conversation and I assumed he felt the same, so we stood in silence a short while. We were from different walks of life, with different backgrounds, knowledge and interests, the only common thing between us being the death of a child, and at that moment we both seemed at a loss what to talk about.

I scanned the room, taking in the other mourners whilst sipping at my sherry when I suddenly caught Edward looking at me suspiciously.

"What's wrong?" I asked.

Edward shrugged.

"Nothin', Mr Attwood." He then tried to act casual. However, that only lasted a second or so before he leaned in close to my ear so that when he spoke his voice was little more than a whisper.

"Alright, Mr Attwood, I have to know. Tell me, the thing with the flower, how did you know about it?"

I was not surprised that there had been such a flower, only surprised that Edward was now mentioning it.

"So, there *was* one left with her body?" I asked. "A lily?"

"There was." The big man kept his voice low. "I don't know why, but there was."

I was about to tell him about Miss Hunter when a group of mourners came and stood right by us and so I remained quiet. Edward guessed why I had not spoken and so he pulled his pipe from his jacket pocket and asked, "You feel like a smoke? Outside, Mr Attwood?"

I said I did and followed the burly man out into the front street, away from any prying ears.

"Mr Chambers told April to get rid of it," Edward said as he lit his pipe. "She threw it out that morning. She found Emily, remember. There was a lily on the poor child's chest, like it had been left there as a sign of respect or somethin'."

"And April told you this?"

"She did. Mr Chambers told her not to speak of it to anyone, but you know how it is, me and her are staff. We talk about things like all workers do. She told me about it the mornin' we found Emily dead. After you mentioned it yesterday, I asked her if she had told anyone else about it and she swore she hadn't."

"So only Mr Chambers is meant to know of it?" I asked. "Not even his wife?"

"Not his wife, not Dr Bernard, not the undertaker, not anyone else. But somehow, you *did* know about it, Mr Attwood. Tell me how."

I lit my pipe and asked, "Have you heard of a woman named Mary Hunter?"

Edward appeared to think for a moment. Then he said, "No, sir. Can't say I have. Who is she?"

"That's just it, I don't really know. She just came up to me on the street and started asking questions about Mr Chambers and Emily. She asked if a flower had been left with the body. She also told me Emily had been killed."

Edward frowned, one eye closing fully due to the smoke bellowing out of his pipe. "Why and how?"

"I don't know that either." I sighed. "But that's not all. A friend of mine, a police officer, investigated a murder last month where a lily had been left with the victim also."

Edward's eyes widened with interest. "Was this one a child, too?"

"No, an adult. An older man." I shrugged, trying to think of a connection but coming up short.

"How did this Miss Hunter know you had business with Mr Chambers?" Edward then asked.

"She saw me here the day I took the photograph. I noticed her when I was leaving."

"*She* was the woman you said you saw?"

"Yes, she came to see me again last night. She said she had been to see Mr Chambers yesterday and he threatened to go to the police if she bothered him again."

Edward nodded to himself. "I think I know who you mean. Yes, pretty young thing. She came to the house yesterday afternoon. I thought she must be askin' for work or somethin'. They spoke at the front door. I was tendin' to the horses, so I saw them but didn't hear what they talked about. However, Mr Chambers didn't look happy with her and sent her away after only a minute or so."

I decided to trust Edward and tell him what Miss Hunter had also told me.

"She said her nephew and Emily had been murdered by..." I was about to mention ghosts when I thought better of it. I wanted him to believe me, not think me mad. "...she said that Emily and her nephew had been murdered for something that their fathers had done."

"Like what?"

"I've no idea."

Edward puffed on his pipe a few times and then said, "So, if her nephew was killed for somethin' his father done, that would make the father this lady's brother, and she is *Miss* Hunter, meanin' that her brother's surname would've been Hunter also."

"I assume so." Then I understood why Edward had said that. "Do you know if Mr Chambers knew of anyone with that surname? A friend? A client, maybe?"

Edward nodded. "Mr Chambers attended a funeral about two weeks back. I didn't drive him there as he said he wanted to walk. I think the surname might have been Hunter, but I can't be sure."

"A funeral? Could it have been Miss Hunter's nephew?"

"I don't know, Mr Attwood. But Mr Chambers went alone so I take it the deceased wasn't close to the family. I also doubt it would be a child, either."

We smoked in silence for a minute or so as I let all this sink in, unsure what to make of it all. Edward then snuffed out his pipe and knocked the excess tobacco from it. Then he asked, "Why would Miss Hunter come here *after* Emily had died? What good would it do? I mean, it seems like lockin' the gate after the horse has bolted."

I thought on this for a moment and then remembered something Miss Hunter had said to me during our first encounter.

"She said she first came to see Mr Chambers a week before Emily died," I said. "I think she was trying to warn him that his daughter was in danger. Her nephew had recently died, and she somehow thought that Emily was going to be next. That's why she came to see Mr Chambers again yesterday. That's why she came to me. She wants someone to help her as she believes that there will be more deaths."

"And how would she know all of this?" Edward asked.

I shrugged. "I wish I had given her the chance to tell me."

Edward folded his arms and appeared to think about what I had said. If he wanted to add to the discussion though, he never had the chance as a few seconds later four black stallions pulled a funeral carriage to a stop outside the house.

It was time to say goodbye to Emily, although I had a strange feeling that I would see her again.

19

A TALK AMONGST THE DEAD

The tombstones in the cemetery behind St John's Church were coated in a fine sparkle of frost and the grass had hardened so that it crunched underfoot as we all made our way to Emily's gravesite. I remained at the back of the crowd, feeling uncomfortable and out of place despite my personal invite. Mr and Mrs Chambers walked directly behind the coffin that was carried by four tall men dressed in black top hats and tails. Behind the grieving parents walked Dr Bernard and others whom I assumed were family members and close friends. Edward and April were in amongst them. Behind them, where I walked, I assumed were neighbours and acquaintances of the grieving couple.

When we all took our place around the grave and the vicar began his speech, my mind wandered off. The last funeral I attended had been that of my father and I had promised myself the only other I would ever attend would be my own. But I felt I had to be here today and despite my feelings of unease I stood strong and silent.

Finally, the coffin was lowered into the grave and there came a mixture of sobs and wails from those closest to the grave as it swallowed the body of the innocent child.

A murdered child, I now believed. But how and why and by whom remained a mystery.

The vicar muttered the last prayer and dirt was thrown on the coffin as a final farewell. Then it was all over. Ten minutes was all it had taken to pay respects to the life of a thirteen-year-old girl.

It seemed so brief.

As we as a group left the gravesite, a crow sounded above us, the shrieking *caw* echoing around the graveyard, foreboding and ominous. I looked up in time to see it take flight above the headstones across the way and, as my eyes followed it, I noticed a solitary figure standing on the highest point of the cemetery, a couple of hundred yards from us.

I stopped and let those around me continue towards the gates of the churchyard. None of them seemed to notice what I was looking at, nor did the two diggers who were now hard at work filling in Emily's grave.

The figure watched me for a few seconds and then turned and vanished over the crest of the hill and I felt a chill run through me as I realised who it was.

I had to follow.

As the last of the mourners left the cemetery and knowing that I would not be missed by any of them aside from maybe Edward, I headed back past Emily's grave and followed the gravel path up the incline.

When I reached the crest and looked down, another acre or so of graveyard spread out beneath me with monuments in the shape of crosses and mausoleums chiselled from marble fanning in a plateau of mourning.

And then I spied the figure again, the black dress and bonnet boldly standing out amongst the background about a hundred yards or so down the slope. It was approaching a small copse of trees that contained a creepy looking Weeping Willow that was twisted and hunched over as if in pain.

The figure - the woman - looked back at me briefly, and even from such a distance I noticed the pretty face and large, sad eyes as I quickly headed down the slope towards her.

As Miss Hunter slowly walked on, she neither seemed concerned by my pursuit nor quickened her pace to flee me.

I lost sight of her for a few seconds as the trees blocked my view but once through the branches, I found her again about fifty yards further on, standing in front of a solitary headstone.

I walked up behind her, my feet crunching loudly on the frozen grass, but she never looked back at me, just at the grave in front of her. The mound looked fresh, as if a burial had occurred very recently. The headstone was older, however, maybe by a decade or so, and was chipped in places and green with moss in others. There were three names on it. The first name was faded slightly, the deceased obviously being the longest resident of this plot.

BELINDA HUNTER
LOVING WIFE OF WILLIAM
MOTHER OF ADAM
FOREVER IN OUR HEARTS
BORN JULY 1830
DIED AUGUST 22 1856

I then read the second epitaph, the chiselled script a lot fresher than the words above it.

ADAM HUNTER
LOVING SON OF WILLIAM AND
BELINDA
TAKEN TOO SOON
SLEEP WELL, CHILD OF GOD
BORN AUGUST 22 1856
DIED DECEMBER 01 1864

I noticed that Adam's date of birth matched his mother's date of death and assumed her to be another childbirth fatality.

The final epitaph read:

WILLIAM HUNTER
WIDOWED HUSBAND
OF BELINDA
DOTING FATHER TO ADAM
BELOVED BROTHER OF MARY
BORN JANUARY 09 1826
DIED DECEMBER 06 1864

Mary's brother was dead also. He had died almost three weeks ago, only a few days after his son. Allowing a week or so for arrangements to be made, I assumed that must have been the funeral that Mr Chambers had attended two weeks back.

"My brother, his wife and their son," Miss Hunter said without looking around at me. "At last, they are together again as a family, and alas, they were the only family I had left."

"I'm sorry for your loss," I replied. Then, I said, "I believe you about Emily Chambers. I think there might be more to her death than her dying in her sleep."

Mis Hunter finally turned to face me, and even the grief she held could not mask her good looks.

"Why do you suddenly believe me, Mr Attwood?"

I was almost about to confess everything and tell Miss Hunter about what had happened during the previous two nights but, in the end, I decided to tell her something more rational.

"There *was* a lily left with Emily Chambers' body," I said. "I just found out today."

Miss Hunter's expression never changed, as if the revelation was no surprise to her.

"I'm sorry that I never gave you the opportunity to talk," I then told her, honestly, "but now I'm ready to listen. Who do you think is responsible for their deaths?"

Miss Hunter did not hesitate to answer.

"A woman," she said. "She was called Angela Parsons."

The name sounded familiar, but right then, in the heat of the moment, I could not think why, nor did I have the time to.

"Who is she?" I asked. "Is she the ghost you spoke of?"

Miss Hunter smiled sweetly and shook her head. "I will not bother you with talk of ghosts again. I did not mean for you to follow me here. I merely wanted to pay my respects to Emily Chambers from a distance as I knew I would not be welcome at the service. I have given up trying to convince people of what I know. You may leave and I shall bother you no more, Mr Attwood."

"Please, call me Charles," I said. "And I want to hear what you have to say."

As I finished talking, the breeze picked up, rattling the skeletal branches of the trees behind us, and with it, for my ears only…

(Help me…)

"Very well, Charles," Miss Hunter said. "Call me Mary. Now, let me take you somewhere and I will explain everything."

With that, she walked off without waiting for me, as if she knew I would follow her.

And follow I did.

20
SECRETS OF THE PAST

We did not speak a word to each other as we left the cemetery. I felt like pressing Mary for more information, especially when we reached the main road and she hailed a hansom cab and asked me to climb in, but I thought it best to wait. If she had wanted to speak by now then she could have, but for some reason she wanted to take me somewhere first. More importantly, I trusted Mary. Only yesterday I had thought of her as being strange and delusional. Now I felt that she was a kindred spirit.

I climbed into the cab as Mary instructed the driver where to take us. After we had been travelling for maybe ten minutes, we pulled up outside a building I had never seen before but knew exactly what it was. More importantly, I knew why the name Angela Parsons had sounded familiar.

The building was a single story, red-bricked hall with a large house behind it, both standing separate from the other houses in the street. It looked unused and in need of repair. The high windows were grimy and thick with dust (at least one of the four I could see was cracked and missing some glass) and there were several tiles missing from the roof. The front door was half-open and rocked on its rusty hinges in the breeze. Above the door was a faded sign.

ST SIMON'S HALL
SCHOOL FOR BOYS

Mary paid the driver as she climbed down to the street.

"I believe this is where it all started," she said and headed towards the building, and by the time I caught up with her she had already pushed the door open fully and stepped inside.

I coughed as dust hit my throat and I strained my eyes to peer though the gloom at the small desks and several chairs scattered about the place. Around the perimeter there were heaps of rubbish including broken bottles, crumpled newspapers, and scraps of food. The place smelled stale and dirty.

"I think homeless people use the hall to shelter during the night," Mary said. "It's been closed for years and so they know they can lay their heads down and not be moved on by the police."

"No, only one person used this place recently," I said. "His name was Arthur Olsen, a Danish immigrant. He was recently found guilty of murdering the man who owned this hall and the house behind it. His name was Jeffery Parsons."

Mary's eyes widened. "I know. I read about it. I take it you did, too?"

"Yes. But the newspaper didn't mention the most important thing. A lily was left with his body also."

Mary's eyes shot open more, this time in definite surprise.

"But what is it about this place that links Emily and your nephew?" I asked. "They were too young to have come here when it was a school."

"But their fathers were not." Mary said. "My brother came here for a year or two when I was very young. My parents wanted to give him a chance in life, and that started with a basic education. Because of it he ended up becoming an apprentice draughtsman, finally working his way up to a high position with a civil engineering firm." She then reached inside her coat pocket and pulled out a folded envelope and handed it to me. "I received this letter in the post the day after my nephew's funeral, the day my brother was found dead by a neighbour who had called to see him. He must have posted it before he took his own life."

"Your brother killed himself?" I asked, surprised by the revelation.

Mary nodded. "He could not go on without Adam and hanged himself in his bedroom. I think he arranged for his neighbour to find him so that I would not. Please read the letter."

I opened the envelope and took out a single piece of paper but could not make out what was written on it because of the gloom inside the hall. I walked to the cracked window where a beam of light was shooting down from outside and soon could see the handwritten words more clearly.

My Dearest Mary,

I hope this letter finds you well despite the stress of this last week. I have been so very grateful for your support since Adam died and you were my rock this morning at his funeral. However, since returning home to my empty house, seeing his clothes that he will never wear again still folded in his room, his bed that he will never sleep in again still made up, and the silence... the depressing silence, they have all made my mood deteriorate to the point that I know life is no longer worth living.

You may think me not of sound mind as I write these words, and you, my sweet, loving sister, may very well be correct, but that does not change the terrible truth that my son's death was my own fault.

I have thought back to my childhood a lot since I found him, asleep forever with the flower placed on his body.

Oh, the lily! The lessons at St Simon's! After years of trying to forget I remember it all so very clearly now, especially the day it all happened. The day we crossed her and sealed her fate. Now she has returned from beyond the grave to seal my own - and that of the others, too, for I know there will be more deaths. Adam was the first I know of, but she will surely come for the other children. She wants revenge for the loss of her own. She wants all of us responsible to suffer in the same manner.

I maybe should try to find them and warn them but what good will it do? How can they stop her? How do you stop a vengeful spirit? I do not know, and that is why my heart is so heavy with despair and I can no longer go on.

Do not show this letter to anyone, dear Mary. They will only think me insane. Be strong and forgive me for what I have done and for what I am about to do. Live a good life. This one ends for me tonight. Do not mourn for me, for death is the only peace I can hope for now.

Your loving brother, forever,
William

I handed the letter back to Mary and did not know what to say. From his writings her brother seemed on the very edge of insanity, and I could understand why she had not gone to the authorities.

"So that explains the connection to this place," I said. "I assume the 'she' he keeps referring to is Angela Parsons. I take it she was a relation to his teacher, Jeffery Parsons?"

"Yes. His daughter."

"How did you find out about her?"

"Because that letter was just the start," Mary said and handed me another piece of paper she took from her coat pocket. This one was brown and crumpled with age.

I took it and noticed it was an old piece of newspaper, from September 1859, five years ago.

"I found it in a box of my brother's belongings the day after his funeral when his house was being cleared," Mary said. "He had kept it, like it meant something to him.

It mentions a fire at an asylum and a lady who was killed there."

Outside, the wind picked up, slamming the open door against its rusty hinges and I jumped and looked. I thought, briefly, that I caught a glimpse of a figure outside.

Emily?

But, once the wind died down and all became silent again, I knew I had been mistaken.

I then began to read.

FIRE HORROR AT MENTAL ASYLUM

Tragedy struck last Sunday at All-Hallows Asylum on the Hoo Peninsular in the county of Kent when a blaze ripped through the building killing several patients and injuring many more. The fire was believed to have been started by a patient, a Miss Angela Parsons, who had been held there for over twenty years. It is understood that she deliberately set fire to her quarters, and the fire quickly

spread until it engulfed most of the West wing of the building causing severe damage and taking the lives of seven patients, including that of Miss Parsons herself. Dr David Halliday, who has recently taken charge of the facility, said, "We have no idea why this patient started the fire. She had been placid and co-operative for most of her time here. It just goes to show that psychiatric problems can return for many inflicted people throughout their lives and shows the importance of institutions such as All-Hallows for the protection of those afflicted and the general public alike."

Angela Parsons had been a patient at All Hallows since April 1837. Her father, Jeffery Parsons, from Westminster, a retired school teacher formerly of St Simon's Sunday School which he ran with the help of his only daughter, had her admitted after she reportedly became psychotic and uncontrollable. Her first year at All Hallows were spent in solitary confinement where she repeatedly swore revenge against her father and others that

she blamed for murdering her child, a child that reportedly never existed. Although a model patient during later years, her role in the fire seems to point to a severe relapse of some kind.

When I finished, I looked at Mary and said, "I take it your brother was one of the people she blamed for the death of her child?"

"Yes, and I believe Mr Chambers also. I did not know of him until he turned up unannounced at my brother's funeral. He said he was an old friend of William's from childhood and had not seen or heard from my brother for years. Indeed, he did not know of my nephew's death and had only heard of William's demise by chance through his work as my brother's estate was being handled by the same company that employs Mr Chambers. After the service, as we talked, he mentioned that he met my brother here, at St Simon's, and when he left, he gave me one of his business cards with his address on it, as a gesture I suppose, in case I required any help in the future. I went to his house after I found the newspaper clipping and showed him both that and the letter, to see if he would tell me what happened all those years ago to make Angela so angry with them, but he claimed to know nothing and suggested that my brother must have simply lost his mind. I did not believe him, but when I begged him to give me some answers and told him that maybe his own child was in danger, he became angry and asked me to leave and never return. I have passed his home on my way to the high street several times since and last Sunday, when I saw you there and the wreath on the door and realised that a death must have occurred, I knew that there must be something to all of this. After all, the sudden deaths of two children of two friends in the space of a couple of weeks? After one of those friends had written about a secret from their past that he was sure was to blame." She shook her head. "That is why I asked you if there had been a rational explanation for Emily's death, like a recent illness. That is why I asked you about the lily. That is why I plucked up the courage to visit Mr Chambers again yesterday to convince him that his daughter's death had not been due to natural causes and for him to go to the authorities. He sent me away as he, like my brother, does not want to think back and face whatever they had done when they came to this place as children. That is why I wanted you to listen to me because I was at a loss what to do and judging by my brother's letter there may be more children who may die. I fear Angela has not finished what she has started."

Something was still bothering me about all of this, the main thing being that according to reports, Angela Parsons was very dead. I believed in Emily appearing to me, but I found it harder to believe that a ghost could physically harm or take the life of someone. And there was something else I could not understand.

"Why the lily?" I asked. "What's that got to do with anything?"

"I am not sure," Mary said. "I assume it is because the lily is often seen as a symbol of death. Its mysterious appearance with the bodies may simply have been a message so that my brother and Mr Chambers would know that their child had not simply died but had been murdered."

I nodded, agreeing that it could be as simple as that. Then I remembered something, something from my art studies when I was younger. Symbolism played a huge part in paintings. The colour a person was dressed in or the hand they held an object in could be used to show some hidden meaning. Flowers were also used that way, and right then I remembered that the lily also represented something else.

"Resurrection," I said, quietly, almost to myself. "The lily is the flower of the resurrection."

"What?" Mary asked.

"The garden of Gethsemane," I said. "The place where Jesus first appeared after the resurrection. Lilies were said to have grown there. They were also said to have sprouted from the drops of Christ's blood as he died on the cross. They are now seen by the catholic church as a representation of rebirth. That's why many churches are decorated with them at Easter, the time of the resurrection." I smiled, thinking I might be close to something important. "The flower is not left with the body as a symbol of death, but as a symbol of life. Maybe Angela didn't die in that fire. Maybe people thought she had but she survived."

Outside, the wind picked up once more and with it came Emily's voice.

(*Help meee...*)

"I think I may know what to do," I then told Mary. "I may know someone who can help us."

21

SEARCHING FOR ANSWERS

It was my turn to hail a cab and I asked the driver to take us to the police station on Victoria Road. As we travelled, I explained to Mary that detective Burke was my friend and had worked on the Jeffery Parsons murder case. He may have delved deeper into the deceased's family history during his investigations. He may know if the news report about Angela dying in the fire was wrong. Maybe she survived, or maybe they did not find a body. All I hoped is that he would tell us something that would point to a human killer, for at least I knew that humans could be stopped.

"But what if there is proof that she really did die?" Mary asked. "What then?"

"Then we are dealing with a ghost," I said.

"And will your friend believe you if you tell him that?"

I smiled and shook my head. "No."

Mary returned my smile and took hold of my hand. She squeezed it gently, as if grateful of my support in such a strange endeavour that we had found ourselves on. I was grateful too. It had been a long time since I had someone show me anything close to true affection.

The cab eventually pulled up outside the station and I quickly paid the fare. I then helped Mary down to the pavement and, without thinking, without even realising, I kept hold of her hand as I led her inside.

A tall, stocky officer in a blue uniform who was sitting with his feet up on the reception desk and enjoying a smoke, quickly tried to make himself appear more professional as we hurried over. I told him that I needed to speak with Inspector Burke urgently.

"Do you wish to report a crime?" he asked, laying his pipe down on the desk and picking up a pencil.

"Possibly," I told him. "Is Inspector Burke in?"

"And who are you?"

"A friend of his," I said. "Is he in?"

The police officer shook his head and said, "I need more than that, sir."

"My name is Charles Attwood," I told him. "Tell the inspector I need to speak to him about a recent investigation. Tell him my name and I'm sure he will be more than happy to see me."

The officer looked from me to Mary and then back at me. Then he said, "Wait right here, please," and left via a door behind the desk.

As we waited, I watched the people going by outside through the window, living their normal, everyday lives. Until two days ago, I had been one of them. How things had changed so quickly.

A minute or so later, the police officer returned, and I was relieved to see my friend Andrew Burke behind him, his shirt sleeves rolled up and his tie loosened. A pipe stuck out from one corner of his mouth. He smiled when he saw me.

"How can I help you, Charlie-boy?" He shook my hand. "Sergeant Peters here said you burst in like a maniac. What's wrong?"

"Can we talk somewhere more private, Andrew?"

"Sure." He looked at Mary and so I introduced her simply as 'my friend'. "What's going on? Peters said you mentioned something about a recent investigation."

"Sort of," I said as he led us through the door behind the desk and into a narrow corridor.

It was warmer in here and there was a heavy fog of tobacco smoke lingering at head height. Burke then showed us into a small room that I assumed was used to interview witnesses and suspects. The walls were plain brown and there was a small window devoid of glass high up towards the ceiling that had iron bars across it. There were only two seats and so I let Mary and Burke have them as I remained standing.

"It's about Jeffery Parsons," I said. "Well, his daughter, actually."

"What about her? She's dead," Burke said.

"Is there any real proof of that?"

Burke frowned. "You're confusing me, Charlie."

I looked at Mary and she nodded, as if to give me permission to continue, and so I told Burke about Mary's brother, about the letter he sent her before taking his own life, and the newspaper report she had found after his death. I handed them to Burke, and he looked them over as I then explained about Emily's death and the fact that her father and Mary's brother were friends who had attended St Simon's school together. I told him that the newspaper report showed Angela was insane and swore revenge against those that she believed had wronged her. Most importantly, I explained that there was reason to believe a lily had been left with both the bodies of Adam and Emily, just like there had been with Jeffery Parsons, and that I suspected it to be a sign for them to think that she had risen from death to gain her revenge.

When he finished reading, Burke handed the papers back to me, folded his arms and sucked on his pipe, his face giving nothing away. Then he chuckled slightly.

"Ghosts, Charlie-boy?" he said. "Is that what you're telling me?"

"No, yes..." I sighed. "I don't know, but I think something should be checked out."

"Like what?"

"Could you find out if Angela Parsons really died in that fire?"

"She did. That's a fact, just as the newspaper states. We checked all next of kin for Jeffery Parsons and his daughter is dead."

"But what if she didn't? She had reason to kill her father as she believed he took her child. We think she had a reason to go after Adam Hunter and Emily Chambers to get back at their fathers for something they had done also. That's why the flower was left at the scene of the three crimes."

"No, it was left at one crime scene," Burke said. "That of Jeffery Parsons." He turned to Mary. "Do you have the lily that was left with your nephew's body?"

"No," she said. "I assume my brother got rid of it."

Burke turned to me. "Does anyone have the lily found with Emily Chambers' body?"

"No," I told him. "Her father told the maid to throw it away."

"So, there is no proof that they existed."

"How do we know about them, then?" I asked.

"Because I told *you* about it, Charlie. Last night, in the pub, remember?"

"Mary told me about it before then," I argued.

"Can you prove that?"

I shrugged and blew out my cheeks. "Well, no. But what about Edward? He works for Mr Chambers. I asked him about the flower, and he confirmed that there was one left with Emily's body."

"So, you mentioned it to him first?"

"Yes, but..." I let the sentence trail off as Burke sat back and rubbed his face, as if he could not be bothered with any of this.

"How did Emily Chambers die?" he then asked.

I shook my head, knowing where this was going.

"A seizure of some sort, but-"

Burke turned to Mary and, ignoring me, asked, "And your nephew?"

Mary looked at the floor.

"The doctor who examined him said he died in his sleep," she said, knowing her answer would not help our cause.

"So, nothing suspicious," Burke said, dismissively. "Look, Miss Hunter, I've seen a lot of bad things in my time with the police force and I know how tragedies can affect people's minds. Your brother was obviously not in his right mental state when he wrote that letter. After all, he took his own life soon after. You're just trying to make sense out of insanity. If I were you, I'd try to forget about it and move on with your life."

"I understand that, inspector," she said, "but if you were in my situation, would you just forget about it and move on."

Burke looked at me and sighed, long and loud.

"You really want me to find out if Angela Parsons is still alive?" he asked.

"Yes, that's all we want," I replied.

Burke smoked a little more on his pipe and looked at me like he did not recognise me anymore. Then he said, "Fine. I'll make a few enquiries." He held out his hand and snapped his fingers. "Give me the letter and the newspaper clipping for reference. I'll see if we have anything on file about the fire. If not, I'll send a telegram to the Asylum and ask for information. With it being Christmas in a couple of days, it might take a little longer than usual, but I'll do it for you, as a friend."

"Just find out if she really died, Andrew," I said. "That's all we need. If she did, then you can forget about all of this."

I thanked him as he showed us out into the reception area again.

"I'll be in touch as soon as I find something," he said when we reached the front door. Then he looked again at the crumpled newspaper report and the letter and shook his head. "Why are you getting involved with this, Charlie? You didn't really know any of the victims and had never heard of Angela Parsons until today. You're a photographer, not a copper. Why is this so important to you?"

Right then, I heard two simple words in my head.

(*Help me...*)

"It's not just important to me," I said.

Then I gently took hold of Mary's hand and led her outside into the cold.

22
CONFESSIONS OF GUILT

"What now?" Mary asked as we walked along the crowded street, heading nowhere in particular. Darkness was once again seeping into the land and the temperature had dropped by several more degrees than it had been at midday and we both shivered as the wind cut through us.

"I don't think there's anything more we can do for the time being," I said. I was suddenly very aware that I was still clutching her hand. To the people we passed, we may very well have appeared a courting couple. Mary must have noticed this too, but if it bothered her then she did nothing about it. In fact, once or twice, I deliberately loosened my grip to see if she would break free from my hand, but to my delight she tightened her hold. "We'll just have to wait until Burke gets back in touch with us and tells us whether we are dealing with a woman or the ghost of one."

Mary nodded and then lowered her head, as if suddenly disappointed.

"What's wrong?" I asked.

She stopped walking and finally let go of my hand. I instantly felt colder and more alone.

"Nothing," she said, crossing her arms over her chest as she shivered. "I suppose it is time for us to part ways, Charles. Time is getting on and I assume you have things to do."

"Not really," I replied, hoping to enjoy her company a little longer. "Do you?"

She shook her head but said, "I suppose I had better head back home and maybe eat something. I have not had much over the last few days. Stress, I suppose."

I asked where she lived, and she told me that it was not far from here.

"I rent a room with three other women who I work with," she said. "Well, used to work with. I was a seamstress at a factory. After I had too much time off after what happened to my brother and his son, I was let go."

"So, what will you do for money?" I asked, generally concerned.

"I have a small sum saved up," she said, "and my brother left me a little in his will. It will see me through until I find something else. Anyway, I best be going."

"Very well," I told her. "I shall wish you goodnight, Mary. And if you ever need me-"

"-I know where you live." She finished the sentence for me, and I laughed.

"Goodnight, then."

"Goodnight, Charles." She turned to walk away and then I thought, *Oh, to Hell with it!*

"Mary," I called, and she turned back. "You said you were hungry. I was going to a place where I usually have my evening meal. I would love for you to join me."

I could tell she was pleased but not surprised at the invite.

"Is this place nice?" she asked.

"No," I said, smirking, "but it'll be a lot nicer with you for company."

She walked back to me and took my hand again. "Then I happily accept, Charles."

*

The pub was quiet as it was not yet four in the afternoon and of that I was grateful. Some of the more unsavoury characters that sometimes frequented the place would not be in for another hour or so when their day's work was done. Mary and I ordered winter broth and bread and she nursed a tin of hot tea while I drank from a tankard of ale more slowly than I would have normally.

"So, you are not married?" Mary asked, making small talk as we waited for our food.

"No," I said. "I never really thought about. I guess I was always too busy with my work. Why did you never marry?"

"I lived with my parents until they died a few years ago. They both had health problems during their later years and so I had to care for them. I suppose because of that I never had the chance to meet someone."

"What a waste," I said, only half-jokingly as the barman brought our food, causing Mary to blush.

We both ate in silence for a while, but I found it hard to enjoy my food as there was something I wanted to get off my chest. Because of the situation Mary and I had found ourselves in, I felt I owed it to her to be fully honest as to why I had agreed to help her. So, I put down my spoon and dabbed at my mouth with my hand before asking, "Remember when we first met, and you warned me that Emily's spirit might not be happy with me photographing her body?"

The question seemed to catch Mary by surprise as she suddenly looked ashamed.

"I should not have said that to you, Charles. I was just frustrated that you would not listen to me. I apologise."

"No, no," I said, "There's nothing to apologise for. But do you really believe in spirits and ghosts and things?"

Mary stopped eating and picked up her drink, more to warm her hands I suspected, as she still looked chilled to the bone. She appeared to ponder the question a moment before answering.

"Yes," she said. "I choose to believe. I have no family left and I find comfort in thinking that this life was not all there was for them – or indeed for me when it is my time. Why do you not believe?"

"I had no reason to, until now," I said.

"Until now?"

Knowing of Mary's belief in the supernatural and that she would not find me foolish, I told her about the two nights I had been visited by Emily who had pleaded for me to help her, and about the lily I had seen on both those occasions also. I finished by saying, "I've tried to convince myself that both incidents were figments of my imagination, but now I'm not too sure."

Mary appeared to mull this over for a few seconds before asking, "If her ghost is real, then why would Emily ask *you* for help? Why not her father or mother? And if she is a figment of your imagination, why would she be asking for help at all?"

I immediately thought back to my time in America, to the event that still haunted my dreams. I then said, "I think I know why."

Mary looked intrigued, and so I took a deep breath and prepared to tell her a story I thought I would keep to myself until my dying day.

"I only arrived back from America a month ago," I said. "I had been out there for almost two years photographing the civil war. I saw some terrible things during that time. The worst thing was only a few weeks before I came home. Indeed, it was the reason I returned."

I shut my eyes, not wanting to think back to it when Mary leaned across the table and took my hand again.

"Tell me, Charles."

I took another deep breath. "I had been travelling with a regiment of Union soldiers for several weeks, heading South in Colorado. One night, during camp, I took ill and had to remain behind while the other men moved on. I think that was probably the worst night of my life. I was alone in the middle of nowhere, delirious with a fever. Luckily, though, I recovered a lot over the next day and night and by the following morning I felt fit enough to set off to catch up with the regiment. About ten miles into my journey, I spotted smoke in the distance and hurried towards it. I knew there was no battle as I could not hear any noise, so I hoped the fire was part of a camp. I was in Union territory and so I assumed whoever I came across would be friendly. As I drew closer though, I saw that the smoke was coming from an Indian settlement. One that had been recently attacked."

Mary looked confused. "Attacked by who?"

"Quite possibly the regiment I had been travelling with," I said, shamefully.

Mary's brow furrowed more as she heard this. "Why would they attack an Indian settlement? I thought the civil war was between the North and South?"

"It is," I said, "but there's still a lot of hostility between the American settlers and the native Indians – especially in that area. You see, a few years back, a treaty was signed between the American government and various Indian tribes that outlined the territory that belonged to the Indians and what belonged to the Americans, but when gold was discovered on Indian territory, the treaty was altered to make most of the gold now the property the Americans. While many of the tribal chiefs agreed to the new treaty and moved on, many didn't, and they and their people remained behind in land that was no longer their own according to official documents. A lot of Americans saw this as an unofficial declaration of war and several violent confrontations took place, resulting in massacres on both sides. When I came across this settlement, I assumed that was what had occurred."

I paused and drained what was left of my ale as I thought back to the sight that met my eyes that morning. I instantly wanted to order another drink and normally I would have, but Mary still held my hand, still looked at me with those large, beautiful eyes and so I did not. Instead, I told the rest of my story.

"I rode closer and even from quite a distance I could see the bodies strewn about the place. The smoke I had seen was from several tents that had been set ablaze and were now reduced to smouldering ashes. I assumed I must have been a day behind the massacre and thought my fever to be a lucky break as otherwise I may have been forced to witness the carnage first-hand. However, despite my disgust, I was out there to take photographs and so I decided to set up my equipment."

Mary exhaled with shock. "You wanted to photograph a massacre?"

"I wanted to capture the reality of war, Mary. I didn't agree with what had happened, but I couldn't change it. All I could do was record it. Anyway, not long after I climbed down from my horse, I heard a noise. It was faint at first and I thought I had imagined it."

"What was it?" Mary asked.

I swallowed hard and said, "It was a baby crying. It came from behind me, about fifty yards away or so. I listened as I walked closer, knowing that I must be mistaken. The sound had to be the wind whistling through the grass or the burnt remnants of the tents. It couldn't be a child. But, as I drew closer to the body of an Indian woman, the noise grew louder. Her arms were out by her side clutching a blanket. I focused in on that blanket and the crying seemed to grow louder, more hysterical. That was when I was sure that I saw the blanket move."

Mary asked, "There was a baby alive there? What did you do?"

I looked her in the eye, ready to tell the most awful part.

"Nothing," I said. "I did nothing, other than mount my horse and ride out of there."

Mary gasped in disbelief, and I fully expected her to let go of my hand and walk out of my company in disgust. However, she did neither.

"You left a child to die?" she asked.

"No," I said, "at least that's what I try to tell myself. There was no way an infant could have survived the attack. I tell myself that it's impossible and that I imagined the sound and that the movement of the blanket was caused by the breeze."

"But what if there *was* a child?"

I shook my head, remembering what was going through my mind that morning. "I was scared, Mary. I was weak and hungry and didn't know how long it would be until I met up with the regiment. I couldn't take a child with me - not one that was possibly injured and starving, and to maybe meet up with the people that might have committed the massacre! What was I meant to do?" I held back tears and said, "If there was a child then I'm paying for my cowardice now. There isn't a single night that goes by that I'm not disturbed by nightmares of that incident."

Mary squeezed my hand, her eyes glossing over also, as if the story had touched her heart.

"And now Emily Chambers is asking you for help," she said. "Whether a ghost or a figment of your imagination, you cannot ignore her. You think you have failed one child and you do not wish to fail another?"

I nodded, slowly, remembering Miss Dawson's story from earlier that day.

"Sometimes it's the person who sees the ghost that is in need of help..."

"Stay with me tonight," I suddenly asked, and it took Mary by surprise.

"Stay with you?"

"You can have my bed and I'll stay downstairs," I said, earnestly. "Emily has visited me these last two nights, you see. I need someone with me, to witness if what I see is real, or if...?"

"Or if you are crazy?" Mary finished for me.

"I was going to say *imagining* things."

Mary giggled and then appeared to think about my offer for a few seconds. Then she said, "If you wish me to, I will be happy to keep you company tonight."

I thanked her.

"You are welcome, Charles." Mary picked up her drink to warm her hands once more. "And I would like to think that you would do the same for me."

"I would," I said, and meant it. "I certainly would."

23

AN UNINVITED VISITOR

Mary and I arrived back at my house by six where I lit the fires and made us a hot drink each.

It was not until I handed Mary her cup and sat with my own that I realised that this was the first night since I had returned to England that I had not brought alcohol back with me to see me through until morning. More than that, I had only consumed two drinks that day (a glass of sherry before the funeral and the ale in the pub) and because of it I felt sober and clear-headed.

We sat in my study and Mary commented on some of my photographs on the wall. Then we chatted for an hour or so, skirting around the obvious tragedies that had brought us together and even shared a laugh or two. In truth, I found it easy to talk to her and I believe she felt the same about me.

By eight, the carollers had returned outside my window. Upon hearing them, I pushed my chair closer to Mary's and we sat watching the coals crackle in the fire and listened to the singing. For the briefest of moments, I felt part of a proper couple. My life felt normal and settled and I wished that what I felt was true.

By nine, Mary looked tired and so I showed her up to the bedroom. It was tidy and the linen was fresh as Miss Dawson had changed it that morning. I also assumed because Mary had no nightwear, that she would sleep fully clothed and so I had no doubts that she would be warm enough throughout the night.

"You should be comfortable in here," I told her. "The mattress is soft, as is the pillow. If you need anything, just give me a call. I'll be downstairs in the study."

"Will *you* be comfortable sleeping on a chair?" she asked.

"No, but then I don't plan on sleeping," I told her. "I intend to stay awake as long as possible. On both previous occasions Emily seemed to appear downstairs first and so I should witness her arrival. I'll then call on you and if you see her, too, then a ghost she must be, and we will try our best to communicate with her. If only I see her – well, I either have acquired a gift of seeing the dead or a very overactive imagination."

Mary let out a small laugh. Then, taking me by surprise, she leant in close and kissed me softly on the cheek.

"*When* she comes, wake me," she said. "Goodnight, Charles."

She then flashed me one last beautiful smile before closing the bedroom door.

I stood outside the room for a few seconds, savouring the sensation of her lips on my face and the lingering odour of her perfume that hovered around me. Then, hearing her climb into my bed, I headed back downstairs to my study where I tried to make myself comfortable.

I added more coal to the fire and removed my jacket, using it as a makeshift blanket as I sat upright in the chair, facing the warming glow of the fire. Every so often I checked my watch to keep track of time. Three o'clock seemed to be the common hour for Emily to visit me and I was sure I could remain awake until then. But of course, as time went by, came the need for rest. I had not slept well the previous two nights and my body craved rest – just as Mary's must have as there had been no noise from upstairs since half an hour after she had retired to bed.

I pulled my jacket up closer to my chin and sank deeper into the chair as the clock passed midnight. Tiredness overcame me slowly but surely. The last time I checked my watch it was a quarter to two in the morning and all was silent both inside and outside the house. After that I remember nothing until I awoke. I did not dream. I did not have time.

*

I sat up suddenly.

The fire had burned out and the room was almost pitch black. A strange sensation was growing inside me that I had become used to, a feeling of something not being quite right, that something or someone unseen had grabbed my attention as I had slept.

I stood up, my jacket falling to the floor as I looked around, my eyes soon becoming used to the darkness enough for me to discern the shape of the hearth, and the edges of my desk, and - as I turned around - the shape that stood by the door.

I knew instantly that it was not Mary. I knew it was not an intruder, either. Not even the most dangerous looking burglar could cause my heart to pound so fiercely and make my breath catch in my throat so I felt I may choke. No, only one person could make me feel like that.

Emily, standing before me, looked exactly like she had in the finished photograph. Her body was the way her father and I had positioned it, with her legs straight, her feet flat against the floor with the base block behind it and her arms hovering out, as if still leaning on her parent's shoulders. Her eyes, although I could see were closed, appeared to have painted pupils hovering ever so slightly from her skin and the artificial stare was focused squarely on me. Her head was still propped up and facing forward with the help of the clamp attached to the central pole I could just glimpse behind her body.

I knew right then that this was no ghost. I had heard stories that so-called spirits often appeared looking the same way they had when they died and often were translucent. But Emily had not died with painted eyes, nor attached to my equipment. My equipment was over there, in the corner of the room. They could not be in two places at once. Also, this apparition had taken on a solid form. I could not see through it to what lay on the other side. So, just what was this standing before me? Was this purely a figment of my imagination? Was this a dream? Had both of Emily's previous visits been dreams too? Whatever this was, I intended to call for Mary and have her come down. If she too saw Emily then all bets were off and a ghost she may well be, but if Mary did not see what I did, if only *I* could see this thing by the door, then I would book myself into the nearest asylum first thing in the morning.

I was about to shout Mary's name when my voice caught in my throat, and I had to cough to clear it.

Then, something I was not expecting happened.

Emily's face, the blank expression, remained the same, but one of her arms moved slowly and stiffly up to her mouth. Her hand tightened into a ball except for one finger, which she placed over her lips, as if to shush me. Then she slowly, mechanically, began to move her head back, and I swear I heard the grinding of the clamp around the base of her skull as she pushed back against it.

She lifted her face towards the ceiling, jerking slightly as she did so, as if looking up to the upper floor. Despite my shock, I also looked, and it was then that I heard the footsteps above me.

When I looked back to where Emily had been standing, she was gone.

Stunned, I quickly opened the study door and hurried out into the hallway. I did not jump or step back when I saw Emily at the foot of the stairs. How she had gotten there so soon and without me noticing (and through a closed door!) was irrelevant. She was there, as if wanting to show me something.

I walked closer and noticed that her position had changed again. She was facing me once more, but her hand was no longer up to her mouth. Instead, her arm was outstretched, pointing up the staircase.

I heard more footsteps above me and looked up the flight of steps into the darkness.

"Help me!"

I heard Emily's voice clearly, the words echoing around the hallway, and when I looked back to where she had been, I saw that she had vanished again. At the top of the stairs, however, I noticed a fleeting shape amongst the darkness. I assumed Emily had travelled unseen again and so, strangely, feeling no fear from this apparition anymore, I hurried up towards my bedroom.

When I reached the top of the flight, I soon realised that Emily was nowhere to be seen again, but that did not concern me.

What *did* concern me was that my bedroom door was slightly open. When I had left Mary earlier, she had closed it fully.

Without thinking too much about it, I pushed the door inwards and my bed soon came into view. Where I should have seen a bulge of covers, with Mary asleep underneath, I instead saw a shadowy figure hunched low over the bed, which I knew was not that of Emily. Then, behind me, the door creaked slightly as it came to a stop against the door frame.

The figure froze for a moment before slowly straightening up, like a wild beast that sensed danger.

"Mary?" I asked. I do not know why. I knew it was not her. I just had to speak.

Then, in a heartbeat, the shadowy thing turned on me and came at me fast, the long cloak and hood it wore making it seem as if it were floating through the air. A high-pitched shriek suddenly came from inside the hood, and I caught a glimpse of two narrow, feminine eyes, the slight glint of light reflecting off them, illuminating the rage and madness they contained.

A woman!

Shocked to the point of collapse, I staggered back out to the landing as the black-clad figure fell upon me and I instinctively spun and pushed it towards the stairs where it slammed headfirst into the edge of the banister.

I heard a satisfying thud of bone on wood and had I been able to put more weight into my defence I am sure my assailant would have been rendered unconscious or even sent tumbling down the staircase, suffering serious injury. As it was, however, the figure soon regained its balance and the hood snapped back in my direction.

I saw another flash of eyes as the thing shrieked again.

Then, before it could come at me a second time, I scurried inside the bedroom, slammed the door shut and sat with my back against it, pinning my weight there with all my might. My heart was pounding, my head was spinning, and I knew that I had just been paid a visit by Angela Parsons.

Seconds later, I heard my assailant quickly descend the stairs, followed by the opening of my front door.

As I sighed with relief that the danger was over, I then realised that Mary would be wondering what was going on. Surely the commotion would have woken her. She should be on her feet, panicking, asking what had just happened.

But she was not.

And when I looked back to the bed, I saw why.

24
A WITNESS TO MURDER

I will be honest and say that I cannot recall much of what happened next. I know that I hurried to Mary and found her lying on her back, her body motionless. Her eyes remained closed as I began to call her name over and over and I checked her wrist for a pulse, panicking more when I did not find one. Then it all became a bit of a blur.

I think I sat by Mary's body for a while. I know I cried. I vaguely remember calling out for Emily, but she did not return (if indeed she had been real in the first place). Sometime later, when dawn began to break and a little light began to filter through into the room, I must have opened the bedroom door and stepped out to the landing.

Feeling like I was dreaming, I walked downstairs and saw that the front door was half-open, so I went outside.

The street was deserted, and I felt like I was the only person in the world. I cannot remember how long I remained out there, my mind blank, my senses obviously in a state of shock. Sometime later, two passing policemen must have stumbled upon me. I explained what had happened and then asked one of them to contact detective Burke, who arrived at my house less than an hour later. Dr Bernard, obviously having been summoned to the scene of a suspicious death to give his medical opinion, arrived not long after my friend.

It was now after nine in the morning and Mary's body had been covered with a medical blanket and loaded onto a cart to take to the nearest hospital mortuary. I sat in my study in a daze, dressed in the previous day's black funeral suit, as Burke talked with the doctor out in the hallway. A uniformed police officer stood guard at the door to the room, watching me with suspicion. Another was positioned outside the front door and I could see through the window that he (as well as the mortuary cart) had attracted many of my neighbours and passers-by who had gathered outside the front of my house.

Soon, Burke and the doctor walked in and stood over me like teachers in front of an insolent child, their expressions a mixture of disappointment and disgust.

"You have to tell me the story again, Charlie," Burke said. "Just so I understand a little better."

So, I did. I explained everything I could remember, only leaving out the fact of Emily's appearance as I was sure that if I mentioned her, it would make my situation worse. I told them that I had invited Mary back here for a hot drink. We sat in the study and talked. Then, lying to save me from telling the truth, I said that she had stayed over because she had felt faint and so I had offered her my bed and I had slept down here in the study. Later, I went up to check on her and was met by a black figure in a cloak and hood at the top of the stairs – a woman – and she fled past me. I then went to Mary and found her dead.

Burke looked at the doctor and raised his eyebrows, as if to gauge whether he believed my story or not.

"There are no injuries to the victim's body," Dr Bernard said. "How did this person-"

"Woman," I interrupted, remembering the feminine eyes I had seen inside the hood. "It was definitely a woman."

And not a ghost!

"My apologies," Dr Bernard said, calmly. "How did this *woman* kill your lady friend? There is no evidence of her death being caused by injury."

"I don't know. I just found her hovering over the body. She must have killed her somehow."

"Why did you go up there in the first place?" Burke asked formally, his position as an investigating officer obviously superior to his position as my friend. "You said you went to check on Miss Hunter. Why? Did something make you think that she might need assistance?"

"Yes, the apparition of a murdered girl alerted me, I thought, but I said, "I heard footsteps up there. I thought Mary had gotten up for some reason."

"And that's when you saw the figure over the bed?" Burke asked.

"Yes."

"Dressed in a black cloak and hood?"

"Yes."

Burke rubbed his chin, thinking. "Was the front door locked before you fell asleep?"

"I believe so." I always double checked it before heading up to bed. Had I forgotten last night because of the change in my routine? Had I allowed Mary's killer easy access into my home? "Anyway, does that matter? The woman got in somehow."

"Even if what you are telling me is true," Burke said, "then how was Miss Hunter killed? Did this intruder – this woman - have a weapon?"

I shrugged, thinking back to Emily, and to Adam, Mary's nephew. Both of those had met the same fate as Mary but the children's deaths had been attributed to natural causes. No cuts, bruises, or marks on their bodies. If the killer was, as I now knew, human, then that could only mean one thing.

"Poison," I said. "They were poisoned."

"*They?*" Burke asked.

"I mean Mary," I said, and Burke looked at the doctor, as if to get a professional opinion.

"It is possible, I suppose," Dr Bernard said after a slight moment of thought. "But it must have been very fast acting." He then looked around the room at my equipment, his eyes drawn to the jars of sensitising and developing solutions on the shelves next to my desk. "I see you have a lot of chemicals in here, Mr Attwood."

I jumped up from the chair, my anger boiling instantly at the nerve of this man.

"Are you implying that I killed Mary? That's absolute rubbish!" I turned to Burke. "You know I'm not a killer."

"I know, Charlie," he said, holding out his hands to calm me until I sat back down. "I know you're not a killer. I think what Dr Bernard is suggesting is that maybe Miss Hunter's death was an accident. You said that you both sat in here and talked a while. Then Mary felt faint, so you offered her your bed. Maybe she was feeling poorly because she may have accidentally inhaled some fumes and later died. Maybe you were slightly overcome with them yourself. Maybe this woman you claim to have seen was a figment of your imagination caused by a slight poisoning that affected your senses."

I shook my head, regretting my earlier lie about Mary feeling unwell, but in no position to retract it.

"No," I said. "Someone else was in the house. I didn't imagine it."

"Alright, if you say so." Burke blew out his cheeks and put his hands on his hips. "You said the door may have been locked when you fell asleep. Did anyone else have a key?"

"Yes, my cleaning lady, Miss Dawson."

Burke asked for her address. I gave it to him, and he wrote it down. "We'll check her out, just to make sure."

"She wouldn't have anything to do with this," I said. "I know who it was. I came to see you about her yesterday. It was Angela Parsons."

Burke sighed and turned back to the doctor. "How long until we have a cause of death?"

"Maybe by this afternoon," Bernard replied, looking at me strangely. "We might find something as soon as we look at her body in more detail, then again we might not."

"Could you check for poisons?" Burke asked. "There're some new tests, aren't there, for arsenic and stuff?"

"Yes, they are not that simple, and the results may take a few days, but we will surely test her for them." Dr Bernard shook Burke's hand. "Anyway, I'll leave you to this police business and follow the body to the morgue. I'll contact you when I have something."

Burke thanked the doctor and Bernard left whilst giving me a look that seemed to be a mixture of pity and contempt. I also wondered if earlier, out in the hall, he had told Burke about my recent visit to his office and the strange questions I had asked. If he had, my sanity would be even more in question by my friend.

When the doctor had gone, Burke asked the police officer at the door to wait with his colleague outside. Then, when it was just the two of us alone in the study, he sighed again, as if exhausted, and sat down in the empty chair next to me. "Charlie, you're going to have to come to the station with me, you understand, don't you?"

"What?" I stood up again and this time ignored Burke's attempts to settle me as I began pacing the floor. "You're my friend and you don't believe me? After everything I told you yesterday."

"Calm down, Charlie, and look at it from my point of view. How will a judge see your story? You believe a dead woman did this. A ghost!"

"I *touched* her," I said. "Angela Parsons is no ghost!"

Burke shook his head. "You don't seem yourself, Charlie. Maybe you've had a breakdown of some sort. The stress of the war... maybe it's sent you over the edge."

"A breakdown would not explain a woman dying in my home without reason. Angela Parsons-"

"Is dead!" Burke shouted, and I was so taken aback by his sudden outburst that I stopped pacing and froze on the spot. He put his head in his hands and rubbed his face, suddenly appearing even more stressed than I was.

I looked at him, confused. Then I remembered something. My friend, Andrew Burke, grew up in a poor household but whose parents had wanted him to get an education and so sent him to Sunday school, just like Mary's brother. I thought back to William Hunter's epitaph, at his date of birth and realised that made them both roughly the same age. Burke was local to the area where St Simon's was located. Then I understood.

"You," I said, in disbelief, and Burke looked up, stared at me, his eyes like a window into his soul. "You're part of this! You're another one who Angela blames!"

25
BURKE'S STORY

"Charlie," Burke warned, "it was a long time ago, and I promise you it's got nothing to do with anything that's going on now. It can't have."

I began to pace the room again, my head spinning. Mary had just been killed in my home. I was experiencing visions of a murdered girl in need of help. I was tired and stressed and I was two days without a proper drink of alcohol. I had rarely felt worse, and now, on top of it all, I had just learned my friend was involved in all of this somehow.

"Andrew," I said, trying to sound as calm as possible, "we're friends, we can trust each other. Please, just tell me something, *anything*, so I can understand what's going on?"

"There's nothing much to tell," he said. "I knew Angela twenty-five years ago, and barely even knew her then."

"And Chambers and Hunter?"

"I haven't seen either of them for almost as long. We briefly went to Sunday school together. That's it."

"At St Simon's?" I asked, knowing the answer. "Where Jeffery Parsons taught with the help of his daughter, Angela?"

"Yes," Burke said, almost ashamed. "At St Simon's Hall."

"Next door to where Jeffery Parson's was found dead? Force-fed poison and left with a lily on his body? And a poor foreign man took the blame for it?"

"All the evidence pointed to-"

"And you didn't make the connection to Angela?"

"Why the hell would I?" he yelled. "I've investigated dozens of messed up murders over the years. Why would I suddenly think this one had to do with the ghost of his dead daughter?"

I almost laughed. "Not even when you found the lily?"

Burke shook his head. "Charlie, you've no idea what happened back then. It was nothing really to do with us. We were just kids. Yes, when I found the lily I thought back to that day, but not for more than a second before I concentrated on finding a murderer who actually existed."

It was my turn to stand over him, as if the tables had suddenly turned and he was now the suspect.

"So, what did all of you do to her?" I asked. "Why is she back killing children?"

Burke seemed unwilling to answer me. But then his face changed, his expression softened to the point that he looked defeated, ready to give up. "Sit down and I'll tell you, Charlie."

I sat down as Burke pulled out a hip flask and drank from it before offering me some. When I declined, he drank some more before putting it back in his pocket.

"I still don't know the full story, Charlie," he then said. "Possibly no one apart from Angela and her father ever did. Like I said, we were kids when it happened, and we didn't know what we were doing. We didn't know what it would lead to. If we were responsible for anything, then it was purely by accident. I've never spoken of this to anyone. Even in the days and weeks after it happened, none of us spoke of it. We were scared, Charlie. Scared of that place, and even more scared of Jeffery Parsons. We were only eleven or twelve years old, from decent families with little money. My Parents, just like the parents of the other kids at St Simon's, wanted us to get an education, so we would have a chance to make something more of our lives other than working at the docks or in a factory. Home schooling and boarding schools were for the wealthy and places like St Simon's offered people in our financial position an alternative. There was about twenty of us boys went there at the time. Jeffery Parsons had money and a good education behind him and so he opened the school as a non-profit organisation and taught us for free. But he had a dark side to him, one that I think was his main reason for opening the school. His wife had a died a few years earlier and he never remarried. He was respected around the community and people assumed he never chose another wife out of love for his first. But us, the kids, the *boys*, we knew differently. We knew his *interests* did not lie with women."

I put my hand over my mouth in disgust. "You mean he...?"

"John Chambers and Will Hunter were the two I became most friendly with whilst at St Simon's," Burke went on, not answering me, as if it was too difficult for him to do so. "The morning sessions were taken by Mr Parsons, where we mainly studied reading, writing and arithmetic. In the afternoons he would select one child to go next door to his office to receive a *personal* lesson, one that you had to keep secret. One that you dare not speak of to anyone. He warned you about that. Most of us, the ones he liked the look of, had at least one of those lessons, some of us more than one. He would take us into the office and teach us for an hour or so. Then he'd offer us food and a drink and take us through this little secret door behind a bookcase that led into his house. I think the doorway was built so that he wouldn't be seen from the street taking a solitary child into his home.

Anyway, once in there, he would do what he wanted to us."

I felt sick to my stomach and instantly understood why thinking back to those days was painful for Burke. That was probably why William Hunter could not face up to his past also. No doubt it was why John Chambers did not want to think that what happened to Emily could be connected to his own, disturbed childhood. But I did ask, "The secret door Olsen was said to have used to get into Parson's house? You knew about it all this time?"

"Yes," Burke said. "When I heard about Parson's murder, I was glad in a way. He deserved it for what he had done to me, to maybe hundreds of boys over the years. But I couldn't tell anyone about that. I didn't want to relive that time. Also, I couldn't tell anyone that I knew how the killer could have gotten into his house and so I had to pretend to find the door during the investigation."

I understood how my friend must have felt, going back to that place after all those years. I had sympathy for him, I really did, but right then I needed to know about Angela, so I asked him to tell me about her.

"During those couple of hours Mr Parsons was away, she taught us religious education," Burke said. "I don't know whether she knew what her father was really up to or not, but I guess that even if she did, she wouldn't have been able to do anything about it. He was a strict man, Charlie, a violent man deep down, and we all felt that Angela was just as scared of him as we were. Anyway, she was about sixteen at the time, four or five years older than us. I suppose she was an attractive girl, but a shy one with it. She struggled to control us boys, as we would often become rowdy during the afternoon, probably because we were relieved that we hadn't been picked by her father for a private lesson. Perhaps it was also because Angela was so shy and awkward and lacking confidence that we knew she would never report us to her father if we misbehaved. Whatever it was, we often tormented her and were flippant and troublesome sometimes to the point where she would be close to tears." He shook his head, as if ashamed. "I believe Hunter, Chambers and myself may have been the worst culprits."

Burke paused to gather his thoughts and I allowed him to. I knew what he was confessing must still affect him deeply and so I did not try to push him for answers.

"It was Easter Sunday when it happened," he finally continued. "It was Angela's last class as we had been told she was leaving to teach somewhere else - some women's institute - I think her father had said. I do remember that we were learning about the resurrection. About the significance of the crucifix and other things."

"Lilies?" I asked.

Burke nodded, solemnly. "Yes, lilies. There was a vase of them on her desk and I remember she started the lesson by explaining their significance to the resurrection. But, that day, I think her mind was not on the job as usually she would lecture us or read from the bible and have us answer questions but halfway through the lesson, she seemed less interested than usual and so had us copy pages from the Bible. Luke, I think it was. Anyway, the three of us - me, Will and John - were bored and for the rest of that afternoon we acted like brats; play-fighting, telling jokes and making fun of Angela." Burke shrugged, his eyes vacant, as if he were staring back into time, to the very moment he was trying to recall. "I think we went further than usual with it being her last lesson. I remember her sitting at the desk trying to write something and getting angrier and angrier at us for being disruptive. Will Hunter said something to her, something rude - I can't remember what, but it must have been something very bad as Angela got up from her desk and stormed over to him. I don't know what she was planning to do; if she was going to strike him or drag him out of the class away from the rest of us. Anyway, we never found out as Hunter got up and ran around his desk away from her, eventually circling around to her desk. We all found it hilarious and laughed as Hunter found a letter she'd been writing and picked it up. He began to read it out loud, mocking Angela's posh accent as she demanded him to stop and raced over to grab him, but he eluded her again and handed the letter to Jon Chambers. Chambers then ran around the room, reading from it also. He even plucked a lily or two from the vase and tossed them at her as she chased him. When Angela nearly caught him, he pushed the letter into my hand, and I ran to the front of the room. I looked at it and found the last part that Chambers had read and was about to read more when I felt a hand clamp down on my shoulder. I turned and saw her father behind me. He must've heard the commotion and had come back through to see what was going on. He had a boy with him who looked relieved to be back amongst the other kids. Jeffery Parsons, however, looked far from happy. He saw us three boys and Angela on our feet and ordered us out of the hall and into the office. He told the other boys to be silent and get back to work, and then he followed us next door."

Burke took another drink from his hip flask. He did not offer one to me before putting it back in his inside pocket.

"Parsons snatched the letter from my hand and read it to himself," he then said. "His face grew white with anger. Then, to our horror, he slapped Angela's face with the back of his hand. I remember that she broke down in tears and asked her father to calm down and let her explain but he struck her again and told her to get in the house. Before she did, she looked at the three of us and said, "Do you realise what you have done?" Burke put his head in his hands. "When Angela left, Parsons then punished the three of us with the cane and told us never to speak of the letter again or we would receive worse."

I remained silent for a while, imagining the scene back then; a terrified daughter and three terrified boys. And one monster.

"What did the letter say, Andrew?" I asked.

"I can't remember it word for word," he said bringing his head from out of his hands and sniffing his nose. "It was addressed to someone she simply called 'My Dearest Love'. That's why Will Hunter had started reading it, because he knew it was very personal and would embarrass Angela. It went on to say something about how everything was in place and that their baby would be born in a safe environment and they would be together again one day. We all understood that she was writing of her own pregnancy but thought nothing of it. Women had children all the time. We didn't know they had to be married and for everything to be legal in the eyes of God. We didn't know her father knew nothing of it until he struck her. Anyway, that was it. Parson's closed the school down the following week. Rumours went around that he had decided to do so because his daughter had a breakdown of some sort and had been sent away to an asylum."

I thought back to the newspaper report Mary had shown me and shook my head. It did not take a genius to guess what had really happened.

"She was placed in an asylum because she had been traumatized by her father forcing an abortion upon her," I said, disgusted.

"Probably," Burke replied.

"And she blamed you three because if you hadn't acted the way you had her father may never have found out."

"I guess so," Burke said. "But can you see how it was not really our fault."

I could. I understood that they had been three children doing what children did. They did not want to get Angela in trouble with her father. They did not know that their actions would lead to the death of an unborn child and scar the young mother for life and break her mind. But none of that mattered. What mattered was that obviously Angela Parsons *did* blame them and she had come for revenge.

"That's why she's after your children," I said. "She wants to do to you what you did to her. She killed her father because he killed her child and she's after your children so that you can feel what she went through."

"She's dead, Charlie," Burke said. "This can't be anything to do with her."

"She's not dead, I saw her last night. I touched her. She's no ghost. I know ghosts and she's not one."

"You know ghosts?" Burke said, frowning. "What does that even mean?"

"Your children are in danger, Andrew," I said, backing away from Burke and edging my way to the door. "Angela is coming for them and I have to stop her."

With that said, I pulled open the door and fled the room.

"Charlie!" Burke bundled after me.

The front door was blocked by the two constables who were enjoying a smoke each. When I ran upstairs and Burke followed, they tossed their pipes to the ground and came hurrying after me also.

I ran into my bedroom and pushed the cabinet in front of the door to barricade it before running to the window - the only means of escape.

As I pulled it open, I could hear Burke shouting after me and then give the order to break the door in after he had no luck trying the handle.

I looked down to the yard below. It was about twenty feet onto the cobbles. I would surely damage myself somehow. Unless...

I heard the first thud against the door and the cabinet bumped away from it slightly. Another hard hit and the door would open fully.

So, I jumped out of the window, aiming for my mobile darkroom below me. The canvas top was soft and would break my fall, but I did not know if I would go crashing through it and smash into the hard wooden floor. But it was a chance I was willing to take.

I closed my eyes just before impact and to my relief my body bounced against the canvas and I rolled sideways before falling the seven feet or so to the cold, hard ground. I did not wait to feel any pain that may come and instead got to my feet and raced out of the yard, only looking back briefly as Burke stuck his head out of the bedroom window.

"Charlie, get back here!"

"Just watch your children!" I yelled. To anyone listening, it must have sounded like a threat and did not show me in the best light, but there was no time to explain otherwise.

When I heard Burke order the constables downstairs to give chase, I kept running, heading West, soon blending in with the crowds on that freezing Christmas Eve morning.

I could think of only one place to go.

26
A JOURNEY FOR TRUTH

"Mr Attwood?" Jonathon Chambers appeared startled to see me at his door so early in the day, out of breath and uninvited as I was. I was wearing the same clothes as yesterday and I had not shaved or even combed my hair. I must have looked a sight.

"Sir, I need to ask a favour of you." I looked over my shoulder, checking I had not been followed, and then realised that might look suspicious and so I tried to act as normal as possible. "You said if I ever needed your help then I only had to ask."

Mr Chambers nodded. "Legal advice?"

"No, sir."

He frowned. "Do come in. But please be quiet as my wife is still asleep. She found yesterday to be most taxing on her."

I did so and remained in the hall despite his invitation for a hot drink in the kitchen. Through the open door, I could see April by the sink, her back to me. Edward was sitting at the table, cleaning the horse reins and looking at me curiously as he did so.

"What is it that you want?" Mr Chambers asked.

"I need transport and would like to hire your carriage and Edward's services for a day, if you have no need for him and he is willing, of course."

"Edward?"

Upon hearing his name, the big man stood up and walked slowly into the hallway.

"I need to travel somewhere on an urgent matter and have no time to book a cab for a return journey," I then explained.

"Where is it you need to go."

"Kent."

The solicitor's eyebrows arched at the mention of the place, as if it held a deep meaning somewhere inside him.

"And it is urgent?" he asked.

"Very so, sir, and I apologise for the short notice."

Mr Chambers frowned. "Mr Attwood, I work in the law industry, and I have learnt to spot the signs of when someone is in trouble. Is what you have planned illegal?"

"Absolutely not, Mr chambers," I told him. "It's just... urgent."

The solicitor appeared to mull this over for a moment.

"I'm willing to pay Edward his day's pay," I said to swing the deal. Luckily, having slept in my clothes, I had enough money on my person to do so. In the end, though, I think it was Edward who helped make up Mr Chambers' mind more than my financial offer.

"I'm happy to oblige, sir," the big man told Mr Chambers. "With permission from yourself, of course."

The solicitor cast me a suspicious glance, but without contempt, as if he knew I was not being fully honest with him but that I must have had a good reason for it.

"Very well," he then said. "If Edward is willing then you may hire him free of charge."

"Thank you." I shook Mr Chambers' hand and reiterated that what was involved was neither against the law nor would it put either Edward or myself in jeopardy. Then I thought, *I hope!*

Mr Chambers said, "I'm glad to hear it." Then he looked at my suit, and at my cold, blue hands. "Do you not have an overcoat, Mr Attwood?"

I looked ashamed and said, "No, sir. I came here in a hurry."

"Then I shall lend you one of mine." He walked to the nearby coat rack and selected a black overcoat and matching hat. He also found me a scarf and a pair of leather gloves.

He handed me them and, thanking him, I quickly put them on.

"The coat may be a little small on you," he said, "but it will keep the cold out. Take care, both of you." He then headed into the living room and closed the door behind him, leaving Edward and I alone in the hall.

"So, when do we leave?" the big man asked, the horse's reins dangling from one of his strong hands.

"Five minutes ago," I said.

*

Mr Chamber's did not see us out and I took that as a sign that he suspected where I was heading and possibly why. After all that had happened, after he had learned of William Hunter's suicide a week after his son's death, after poor Mary had shown him the letter and the newspaper clipping, and surely after the death of Emily with the lily placed on her body, he must have wondered if Angela – either alive or in spirit – had been responsible. I could also, however, understand how he did not want to acknowledge it as fact.

Edward quickly readied the two mares and opened the door to the carriage for me, but I politely declined his offer and asked if I might sit up front with him as I noticed the seat was big enough for two.

"Why of course, Mr Attwood. If you'd like."

"I would." The truth was, I felt the need for friendly company right then and the thought of several hours on the road, alone in the carriage with only my thoughts, was a little unnerving. "And please call me Charles."

"Right you are, Charles," Edward said and climbed up into the driver's seat. "Wrap up mind. It'll be mighty cold, I think."

I turned up the collar on Mr Chambers' coat (which fit better than expected) and climbed up beside the bigger man. A few seconds later, we were off, the horses trotting along the cobbles, heading East.

I made small talk to be polite as Edward steered the horses through the wintery streets. I asked about his family and if he did not mind taking me on such a journey the day before Christmas.

"Oh, not at all, Charles," he replied. "My family is the people I work for, and April, of course. I never had a wife or kids myself. Sometimes I feel sad about that but when things like Emily's death happen it makes me realise that I'm lucky I'll never suffer the pain that Mr and Mrs Chambers have. Hope that makes sense."

I nodded. "I suppose it does."

As we came to Westminster Bridge, I noticed a couple of police officers on foot and I instinctively covered my face with the scarf as we passed.

Edward must have noticed.

"I'm not normally a person to ask questions, Charles," he said, "but will you allow me to?"

"Of course," I said, relaxing a little more as the policemen disappeared behind us.

"Have you broken the law?"

"No," I said.

"Do the police think you have?"

That was a tough one to answer. My friend, Inspector Burke, deep down, no doubt knew of my innocence. But in reality, I *was* a suspect in Mary's death.

"I'm not sure," I told Edward and he nodded, as if he understood, but I failed to see how he could.

"So where exactly am I taking you?"

I told him the Hoo Peninsular in Kent. A place called All-Hallows Asylum.

"Never heard of that place, Charles," he said. "But I know the way to the East-coast. I shall find it though, don't you worry. Are you going to visit someone there?"

"I hopefully wish to speak to someone about a patient there."

"I see. Do you know the patient?"

"Not personally."

"And I take it this has somethin' to do with what happened to Emily?"

"Yes," I said, and felt that Edward needed full disclosure. So, I explained everything apart from the ghostly visions I had witnessed. I told him about the connection of Jonathon Chambers, William Hunter, and my friend Andrew Burke to St Simon's School and all that had happened there. I told him about Mary's letter and the report in the old newspaper. With my voice breaking, I told him about Mary's death. I ended with the fact that I thought Angela Parsons was still alive and responsible for the murders.

Edward did not interrupt once. He never questioned anything I said, not even when I finished. All he did say was, "Why not sit back and try and rest, Charles. You look tired. Don't worry about nothin', though. I'll get us to where you wish to go."

I thanked him and tried to do as he had suggested, but rest, I could not.

A little over two hours into our journey and surrounded by fields on either side, Edward said that he thought we were close to halfway and so we stopped at a country inn to rest the horses and let them drink and eat. Edward and I did the same, although I had little appetite and wasted most of my food.

"So," Edward said, with a mouth full of potato, "if you think this Angela woman is still alive, why are we goin' to this asylum. If she's responsible for the deaths, then she can't still be locked up there."

"I know that," I said, drinking from my mug of tea. Despite my cravings, I had decided to stay off the alcohol to keep a clear head. "My plan is to visit the asylum and see if I can speak to someone there. See if I can find any information that may suggest that the news of her death had been wrong."

"And how are you goin' to do that, Charles?" he asked, dipping bread into his gravy. "Just plannin' on walking in and askin' them to give you all this information, are you?"

"Yes," I said. "If I have too."

Edward nodded. "Very well."

On the second leg of our journey, I sat inside the carriage and this time I tried to sleep but again I could not. Every time I closed my eyes, I saw Mary the way I had last seen her, her face peaceful and serene, asleep forever. I felt like crying but stopped myself from doing so. Soon, instead of grief, I felt more anger than anything. I *was* going to find the truth about Angela Parsons, and I *was* going to avenge the deaths of those she was responsible for. I had to.

After another three hours or so on the road and the sky darkening, I leaned out of the window and ahead of me I could see the haze of the sea. There was marshland on either side of us and hardly any foliage apart from reeds and shrubs. A thick fog hung low to the ground and the air smelt both of earth and sea.

"Not far away now, Charles!" Edward shouted over the sound of the pounding hooves and turning carriage wheels.

A few minutes later, I saw the outline of what I assumed to be All-Hallows Asylum dominating the skyline on a high peak close to the coast about a half a mile away, its grand scale very apparent even from such a distance.

Edward stopped the horses.

"Is that the place, Charles?" he asked.

"I think so," I said, leaning my head out of the window and staring at the Gothic pointed roof, several creepy turrets and thick chimney stacks. "Spooky, don't you think?"

"I do," he replied. Then he looked down at me, his beard frosted white in places. "You need me to come in with you?"

I smiled. "Would you?"

"I would."

"Thank you, but I'll be fine by myself." I then saw that not far ahead of us, another road split off from the one that led up to the asylum, bearing left. A staked wooden sign indicated that it led to the village of Maerfield. "Edward, head to the village. See if you can find us a pub or an inn. You can stay there, and I'll head up to the asylum on foot."

"You sure?"

"I am." Yes, I felt I had to do this alone. Edward had already done more than enough and deserved a rest.

"Suits me, Charles," he then said, staring back at the intimidating structure in the distance. "That suits me just fine."

A few hundred yards further along the road, we passed a small church and several cottages before coming across an inn called The Red Lion. It was small and cosy looking with a painted white facade, thatched roof, and archway door. We paid for the horses to use the stables for food and rest and then went inside.

The inn was warm and quiet, with maybe eight or nine people scattered about the few tables, all of whom were probably regular customers who lived in the nearby cottages. At least one of them, I noticed, was the local vicar, his dog collar a dead giveaway. All were polite and friendly towards us even though strangers were probably rare this time of year.

I handed Edward some money to get something to eat and drink while I was gone and was about to head for the door when he asked, "What are you goin' to tell them when you get there?"

"Anything that will get me inside and find out the truth," I replied.

"Be careful, Charles."

"Careful of what?"

"The truth," he said, and then ordered a beer from the landlord who, out of what I took to be politeness, asked me where I was heading.

"Up to the asylum," I told him, feeling no reason to lie.

"You're going up there at this time on Christmas Eve, sir?" He was a plump, jolly-looking fellow with a huge red nose. I guessed that out of all the beer that was consumed on the premises, he drank the most. "Are you visiting someone?"

"Sort of," I lied. "I have to speak with a doctor up there."

"Oh, right," the landlord said. "Well, if you have any trouble at the gates tell old Jim that if he doesn't let you in then he's barred from here."

I frowned as he and a couple of nearby patrons chuckled. "Who's Jim?"

"My brother-in-law," the landlord replied. "He works as a guard up there. Just tell him you know Harry from The Red Lion and he'll be alright with you. He can be a bit miserable sometimes."

"I'd be miserable if I was married to *your* sister," one of the patrons by the fire said, causing the regulars to laugh even harder.

I smiled and thanked the landlord (who seemed to take no offense at the jibe towards his sibling) and told Edward I would be as quick as I could.

Then I headed out into the cold and fog, and into the unknown.

27
ALL-HALLOWS

I bunched up against the biting cold as I headed out of the village and soon found the road that led up to the asylum. After a few minutes of keeping a steady walking pace, my breathing was heavy and my breath clouded in front of my face, ghostly and ethereal. The creeping darkness filled me with dread and the only sounds were that of my feet crunching into the hardening dirt and the wind that whistled through the marsh reeds on either side of the road. Every now and then I thought I glanced what appeared to be the shape of a young girl dressed in red off to the side of me but each time I looked I saw nothing but rugged nature. All the while, as I hurried onward, the foreboding structure of the asylum loomed closer.

I wondered what the patients who were brought here thought as they rode up this track, looking at what would probably be their home for the rest of their miserable lives. No doubt many of them thought nothing, as they were genuinely disturbed souls. But not all of them. Not Angela.

What had she thought when she first saw this place?

Had she resigned herself to her fate?

Or, from the start, had she planned to escape and seek her revenge?

That thought chilled me more than the weather, and soon – almost too soon – I reached the large, iron gates that surrounded the asylum grounds. A few seconds later, a guard came out of a small wooden cabin to meet me. He was a thin man in his fifties, dressed in a heavy coat and woollen hat. He looked colder than I and not in a good mood.

"Can I help you?" he asked.

"I hope so," I said. On the way here, despite feeling cold and unnerved, I had also been thinking of a decent story to help get me inside. "I'd like to speak with whoever is in charge."

"Are you here to visit someone?" he asked. "Only we extended the visiting times until five this evening. I'm afraid you're half an hour late. I'd have to get special permission to let you in."

"No, no, you misunderstand," I told him politely. "I just need to speak with whoever is in charge."

"You mean Dr Halliday?"

"Is he in charge?"

"Yes, he is."

"Then yes, I would like to speak with Dr Halliday very much."

The guard leant closer to the gates and if it were not for the iron railings separating us, we would have almost been face to face.

"I take it you don't have an appointment then," he said, a statement more than a question, and I was reminded of my attempts with Miss Grainger to persuade her to let me see Dr Bernard two days before. It suddenly seemed like an age ago.

"That's correct," I said. "Please, just ask him if I may speak with him briefly."

"And who shall I tell him wants to speak with him."

"Charles Attwood."

"And that's you, is it?"

"Yes, I'm a photographer," I told him as I thought it would be nice to be a little honest at least.

"A photographer?"

"Yes," I said and then went on with a whopper of a lie. "I'm travelling the country working on a portfolio that may eventually lead to an exhibition. I'd like to photograph this building."

"Tonight?"

I laughed out loud, theatrically. "No, not tonight. Some other time. As you can see, it's quite dark and I have no camera with me."

The guard frowned, eyeing me suspiciously. "Why do you want to photograph an asylum?"

"For a portfolio of work," I said. "It's a magnificent building. I bet the inside is even nicer. May I please speak with Dr Halliday. Just for a moment."

The guard did not seem interested but asked, "How did you get up here anyway?"

"I walked."

"Walked? Where from?"

"The Red Lion," I answered with a smile. "Harry, your brother-in-law, sends his regards."

The guard returned a little smirk back. "Does he now? Fat old drunk." He then sighed and looked at his pocket watch. Then he said, "Follow me."

He cranked open the gates and led me up the narrow path to the front door. I noticed the lawns to the right of us were neat and tidy and that there were several chairs and benches placed here and there. To the left of us, a grass verge sloped away towards some iron railings that sectioned off another area of the grounds where I could just make out the shape of a smaller building.

"What's that down there?" I asked.

"The chapel and graveyard. The ones that die here need to be put somewhere," the guard said, coldly.

As we got closer to the main building, I noticed that the top part of the West wing appeared newer than the rest. The bricks were brighter and neater, the windows slightly smaller and the roof tiles a different size.

"What happened there?" I asked, knowing the answer.

The guard looked up. "Oh, that? We had a fire about five years ago. Gutted the whole top floor on that side."

"Goodness," I feigned. "Anyone hurt?"

"Some patients died. No one really important."

I tried to ignore the guard's cruel remark as we reached the large front door. Above it, engraved in the stone, was a motto which read:

THE MIND IS BUT AN EXTENSION OF THE BODY

The guard opened the door and it swung inwards on creaking hinges that echoed about the place. As we went inside, the warmth hit me instantly. I felt my face flush and the feeling start to return to my extremities. We were standing in a large, clean room. The walls were pristine white, the windows large and leaded, and a collection of photographs and paintings were hung here and there to break up the monotony. Directly in front of me was a huge staircase that split in two directions as it reached the first floor where I assumed the patient's rooms to be located. I heard no crying or screaming, as I thought I might. It was all very calm and quiet, and the place smelled chemically clean.

The guard introduced me to a nurse who was sat at a small desk close to the door and explained my reasons for being there. The nurse (after shooting me the confused look I had become accustomed to these last few days) then asked me to wait a moment before she hurried off somewhere up the staircase. I went to one of the windows and looked out onto the grounds, the guard not far away, silently watching me. From here I could see the cross on the top of the small chapel and rows of graves on the lawn outside of it.

Is there a grave there for you, Angela? I wondered. *And if so, is there anything in it?*

Five minutes later the nurse returned with a short, balding gentleman in his early sixties. He wore spectacles and a white medical jacket, and he cast me a friendly smile as he offered his hand.

"I'm Dr David Halliday," he said. Then, sounded curious, he added, "I believe you wish to speak with me about some photographs or something?"

Since arriving, I had worked on my invented story of photographing the building some more, hoping that I had discovered a way to turn any potential conversation towards that of Angela Parsons.

"Yes, sir, if I may." I introduced myself and explained that I was just passing through the area on my travels back to London and had heard of the asylum through a family link. My uncle was a Mr Jeffery Parsons, whose daughter, my cousin, had once been admitted here, and so I felt compelled to visit. I know I was taking a chance, but I hoped that the news of Jeffery Parsons murder had not yet made the papers outside of the capital.

"Oh, you were related to Angela?" he then asked, apparently convinced of my story from the start.

"I was," I said, feeling no guilt at lying so brazenly. "Such a tragic waste of a life. I guess you could say that was why this building holds a fascination with me."

Dr Halliday smiled in pity. Then he told Jim, the guard, that he may leave us as we both took a seat away from the nurse's desk so that we could talk in private. He offered me a hot drink which I declined and then asked, "So, what will be the purpose of these pictures?"

"An exhibition," I said, impressed by how easily these fibs were rolling off my tongue. "I've already held two in London. My last one was of the civil war that is still raging in America. I saw a lot of death and sickness out there and I think that must have inspired my next project. This one will be about health institutions and hospitals. I also intend to include notes about the history of each place I photograph to tell a more complete story."

The doctor nodded and said, "That sounds very interesting."

"Would you allow the photographs to be taken?" I asked, still acting as if that was my sole purpose for coming. I really wanted to switch attention to Angela and the fire, but I knew I had to bide my time.

"I would have to speak with some other people first," Dr Halliday said, politely. "I am in charge here on a day-to-day basis but there are benefactors on the outside who may need to be informed, but I do not think it would be a problem. As you can see by our walls, we have had photographs taken of the building and grounds before, but of course they were for our own use and not for a public exhibition. However, I certainly would be in favour of such a thing. People have sinister ideas of what an asylum or sanitorium is like and as you can quite clearly see, Mr Attwood, most of them are wrong. The patients who come here, very much like your cousin did, require help, not torture. Here we advise a healthy diet, plenty of exercise and fresh air, with therapy from doctors who want to get to the route of a patient's problem and not simply experiment on them or drug them until they stop showing symptoms of insanity. That is also why we are one of only a handful of facilities in the country to offer family members the right to visit the patients here, so as not to cut them off completely from the outside world."

I saw my opportunity. He had mentioned Angela and so I could not let the chance go.

"I only wish I had known my cousin," I said, faking sadness and nostalgia. "Can I ask about the fire, the one in which Angela perished? I saw from the front of the building that the result of it has changed the facade very much. I would like to include why it looks different in the written notes beside any such photograph I may take. As a family relative, do you think I would be allowed to include the personal nature of Angela dying in the tragedy?"

Dr Halliday seemed to ponder this a moment before saying, "The news of her death is in the public domain, Mr Attwood. There is no breach of confidentiality there. As for other patients and their stories however..."

"I take it there are many tales hidden within these walls?"

"Enough for several exhibitions!" The friendly doctor laughed heartily, and I joined in, fraudulently.

"If permission for the photographs were allowed," I said, "I would only require basic information to put the images into some sort of context. My overall aim is to show the good work people in institutions such as this do."

"Why, thank you, Mr Attwood," the doctor replied, and I realised we were in danger of straying off subject once again, so I pressed on.

"May I ask what she was like – Angela, my cousin?"

Dr Halliday smiled and fiddled with his spectacles. "I had not worked here long when she was first admitted but I remember her well. For most of her stay here she was calm and well behaved, but she was quite hysterical for the first several months of her stay. You know why she was sent here, of course?"

I nodded. "The story told in my family was something to do with the loss of her baby."

"The delusions about a phantom child, yes."

I frowned. "Phantom child? I'm sorry, I've not heard that term before."

"Angela thought she had lost a child when in fact she had never been pregnant in the first place. That is why her father had her sent here."

I then realised that even the people who were meant to care for her did not even know the truth. I had assumed that they had been aware of the forced abortion and Angela had been sent here for them to help her cope with the grief. Now I knew that they just assumed her to be insane, that she had never been pregnant in the first place.

"So, she thought she had been pregnant?" I asked. "That was all it took for her to be admitted here?"

"No, no," Dr Halliday said, "not just that. She was under the impression that her father had killed the child whilst it was still in her womb. All nonsense of course. Her father was a God-fearing man. Besides, Angela was not in a sexual relationship so she could not have been pregnant. The poor child was delusional, and she never got over that delusion. Even during the many years that she was a model patient, she never changed her story."

"I see." I sat for a moment, taking all this in. Then I decided to get right to the point. "Why would Angela start the fire? I mean, if she had been here many years and seemed quite placid for most of that time, why would she suddenly do something like that?"

Dr Halliday shrugged and said, "Sometimes people relapse, Mr Attwood. We have had cases in the past where patients have not had a manic episode for years only for them to suffer a relapse for very little reason. I believe it was something small that triggered Angela's final breakdown. She had been comfortable and trusting with a doctor who had looked after her for most of her time here but who was leaving to work elsewhere. I think she either saw this as a sign of rejection and set out to end her life or it was a cry for help to make the doctor stay and look after her."

I nodded, as if I understood. "May I ask who found her body?"

"A staff member did after the fire was extinguished and we were doing a check of the building. She was still in her room. We believe she started the fire by using a candle to set her bedclothes alight and never even attempted to escape the flames."

"And they could tell it was her?"

Dr Halliday could not help but smirk. "Why, who else could it have been, Mr Attwood?"

"Yes, I mean but did it look like her?"

The doctor sighed and said, "Mr Attwood, you will not like the answer to that question. Have you seen what a fire can do to a person?"

I let that line of questioning go and then asked, "Is she buried here?"

"Yes," the doctor said, respectfully. "Her grave is out by the chapel. Anyway, I am sure you do not wish to use all of this in the exhibition, Mr Attwood. The information is somewhat personal to yourself and your family."

I had almost forgotten about my so-called reason to visit and so, feeling that this had been a wasted journey and that I would find nothing more to help me here, the conversation drifted back to my photography, though I had no interest in the subject and cannot remember what we discussed.

I had failed in my mission.

Angela Parsons was dead, obviously, and whoever was responsible for Mary and the others' murders was still a mystery.

After another few minutes of mindless chatter, I thanked Dr Halliday for his time and told him that I would contact him in the new year to go over more details about the exhibition – which I would not – and he seemed very eager for the non-existent exhibition to go ahead.

As he showed me to the door he then said, "And of course, if you would allow us a couple of pictures for our own little collection?" He held his arms out, indicating the paintings and photographs on all four walls.

"Of course," I said, more concerned on what else I could do before the police found me.

"Actually, this one may interest you." Dr Halliday stopped by an ambrotype photograph of a group of people that was hanging not far from the front door. It was faded and cracked, as could often happen to the collodion process when used with a glass plate.

I leaned in and looked at the date engraved in the little brass plate embedded within the wooden frame.

1859.

The year of the fire, I told myself.

The photograph showed a group of both staff and patients. I could tell that the doctors were the men wearing suits as the male patients wore loose fitting white clothes. The women were harder to distinguish from each other as the white apron of the nurses appeared similar to the uniforms of the female patients. Some of those in the photograph were sitting and some were standing. None were smiling due to the long exposure time. The ambrotype itself was slightly under-exposed, the dark shades not as bold as they should have been and the faces too light and a little blurred, causing them to almost blend with the hue of the wall behind them. However, the quality was good enough for two faces to stand out. One belonged to the doctor standing beside me. The other came as a great surprise to see.

"I know that gentleman," I said, pointing to a man standing at one end of the back row. "That's Dr Bernard. His office is not far from me in London. He worked here?"

"Yes, for many years," Dr Halliday said. "He was the doctor I told you about, the one Angela felt comfortable with. He came here shortly after she was admitted, not long after he had completed his studies to learn more about psychiatry as a primary interest."

I could not believe what I was hearing. I thought back to my first meeting with Dr Bernard, how I acted strangely, and how he told me he had experience with mental health patients. I had no idea it had been because he had worked here, the place where Angela Parsons had been sent.

I studied the picture more closely and soon found another face I recognised.

It was a lady, in the front row.

"And that's his assistant, Miss Grainger," I said, pointing to her. "She still works with him."

Dr Halliday smiled. "I am afraid you are confused, Mr Attwood."

"No, it is," I said. "I've spoken with her recently."

The doctor chuckled to himself and said, "The human brain is a funny thing, Mr Attwood. You have come here and asked questions about your cousin. She is obviously still on your mind because that is who you are pointing to. That is why I wanted to show you this photograph, for Angela is in it."

"What?"

Dr Halliday pointed to another woman in the picture, a lady of a similar age and build to the person that I was sure was Miss Grainger and not Angela Parsons. "*That* is Miss Grainger. She left with Dr

Bernard the day after the fire for him to take over his father's practice in London. The person you pointed to, the one you are mistaken about, is Angela Parsons."

I stood there, stunned.

I think I had found what I had come here for.

28
A RACE BACK TO LONDON

I hurried back to The Red Lion under a sky that was becoming heavy with thick white clouds. I knew snow would not be long in coming and by the direction of the wind, blowing East to West, if we left for London right away the weather would follow and maybe catch us. But after what I had discovered we *had* to leave right away. Time was of the essence.

I burst into the inn like a madman and the landlord and the few other patrons still scattered about the place gave me a startled look. Edward was sitting alone by the fire, nursing a tankard of ale and he paused with the drink to his lips upon seeing me.

"We have to leave now," I told him, quietly.

"Leave for where?" he asked.

"We have to get back to London. Will the horses make it in one trip?"

Edward thought for a moment and then nodded. "I can make them if I have to."

"And you? Are you fit to drive back right away?"

Edward slugged back what was left in his tankard and wiped froth from his bristly top lip. Then he stood up, straight and strong. "The few I've had have barely touched the sides, Charles."

I smiled. Good old Edward.

"Let's get the horses readied and leave," I said.

"And then will you tell me why the hurry?"

"Yes, once we're on the road."

*

We were on the main route back to London ten minutes later, the clouds chasing us and the wind biting and nipping at both myself and Edward next to me, the reins gripped in his meaty hands as the horses pushed themselves to top speed.

"Dr Bernard is behind all of this!" I shouted above the noise of the pounding hooves.

"Bernard?" Edward yelled back. "How? And Why?"

"Not just Bernard but his assistant! *She* is Angela Parsons! I think Bernard rescued her from the asylum! The fire was a distraction and I think the body that was found in Angela's room was his real assistant, the *real* Miss Grainger!"

"And Bernard is the one killin' the children?" Edward asked.

"No!" I yelled. "Angela is the one doing the killing! She's the one I found in my house! Dr Bernard must be giving her the drugs to poison the victims! That's why there are no marks on the bodies!"

"And with him bein' a doctor he can then lie about the cause of death afterwards!" Edward said, adding to my theory.

"Exactly!"

"So, your friend, the policeman?"

"Inspector Burke!"

"Do you think she'll go after his children tonight?"

A shiver suddenly ran through me that had nothing to do with the weather.

"Yes, I think so!" I told him. "Bernard heard me speak of Angela this morning at my house! He knows I suspected her and so they may decide to speed up their operation before I find out more! That's why we have to hurry!"

And hurry we did.

Edward pushed the horses to their top speed as the snow started to fall thick and fast around us.

29
THE LAIR OF THE GHOST

We made the return journey in one stage and arrived back in London not long before midnight. The poor horses, despite the freezing weather and the snow that had travelled with us, were sweating and panting by the time we arrived, and I felt sorry for them. But Edward had had to push them to their limit, regardless of their fatigue and the inclement weather. Lives were at stake!

Ideally, I would have gone straight to Burke's house and told him all I had found out but, alas, he had never given me his new address. I could not go to the police station either as they would hold me there until Burke came, and that was the last thing I wanted. His wife and children would be left alone then, with a dangerous maniac possibly on her way.

There was only one other thing I could think of.

I directed Edward to Dr Bernard's office but, to err on the side of caution, I had him stop roughly a hundred yards from the premises, for I did not want the carriage and horses to alert either his or Angela's attention.

I left Mr Chambers' overcoat, hat, gloves, and scarf on the seat beside Edward for him to return for me, just in case I never got the chance to do so myself, then I quickly jumped down from the carriage, my feet crunching into the laying snow.

"You go on ahead to the police station," I told him, rubbing my hands together to warm them as snowflakes the size of half-pennies floated down around me. "Tell them where I am and that it's imperative that inspector Burke should know. Tell them my name and that I'm a suspect in a murder enquiry. They'll come then."

"To arrest you?" Edward asked. "What good'll that do?"

"I don't know," I said. "Hopefully, I can change their minds when they get here."

"And if you can't, Charles?"

I shrugged. "I have to stop Angela from going to Burke's house. Go on to the station and thank you again for all you've done."

"Should I not stay with you?" he asked. "You might be walkin' into danger and be in need of assistance."

I reached up and shook the big man's hand. "The best help would be to get the police, Edward."

He pushed out his bottom lip, as if contemplating something deep, before nodding in agreement. Then he ushered the horses away, leaving me alone in the dark and deserted street as I headed towards Dr Bernard's building.

There was no sound to be heard except for the crunching of my footsteps and every window on every building I passed was dark, including the one in Fenwick and Son's Bakers that I had photographed two days ago. However, after stopping at the steps to Dr Bernard's premises, I could see a faint glow of candlelight somewhere inside.

They were in there. Bernard and Angela. Awake and plotting.

I stared at the doctor's office for a moment as the nearby church bell rang for midnight and the building took on a menacing form, the windows becoming evil eyes and the door a horrid, vicious mouth. It was now officially Christmas day, a day for most people to forget about work and spend time with their loved ones. I could not help but feel envious of their ignorance to my situation. But I also knew this night would be one of the most important of my life and I had to see it through to its conclusion, whatever that conclusion may be.

Once the church bell stopped, I took a deep breath and headed up the steps to the front door.

And suddenly there she was.

Emily, standing in the now familiar pose, her body still propped up by my equipment, her eyes my painted handywork, but her mouth, her lips…

Maybe it was a trick of the moonlight or the falling snow that did not seem to land on her nor pass through her, but Emily appeared to be smiling.

I did not step back in fear. Goosebumps did not rise on my skin. My heart did not stop beating and my breath did not catch in my throat. I felt nothing other than the certainty that the persons inside this building were responsible for her death and I was about to tell this apparition just that when her image suddenly flickered, like a candle flame caught in a sudden draft and she vanished. In the blink of the eye, the doorway was clear again.

I tried the handle and was not surprised when the door pushed inwards easily. Despite feeling that Dr Bernard and Angela Parsons were expecting me, I stepped into the gloom of the empty waiting room. The door to the doctor's office was closed and the assistant's desk empty. Behind it, the door to the private residential quarters was open and that was where the soft light was spilling out from.

So, walking with purpose, I headed into Dr Bernard's personal residence and soon found myself in an expensively furnished living room. It felt eerie and ominous because of the flickering candlelight, and no doubt because I had a feeling that a killer might be lurking somewhere nearby and may jump out and attack me at any moment. The loud ticking of the clock on the wall echoed off the four walls deafeningly and as I looked to my left where the clock was, my eyes were drawn to a small bottle of clear liquid on a nearby cabinet. There was a glass needle beside it, filled with a similar clear fluid.

Beside that were two white lilies.

Jeremy and Jacob! I thought. *Burke's children!*

As I moved in for a closer look, from the far corner of the room, a deep voice suddenly said, "It is very potent but also very quick and therefore the pain is over soon, if that makes you feel better."

I straightened and walked further into the room, staring at where the voice had come from. Dr Bernard was sitting in an armchair, the right side of his body partially illuminated by the three candles in a stand on the table beside him. He was dressed in a shirt and waistcoat and his bow tie was unknotted so that the two ends hung around his neck, loose and limp, like a dead snake. His legs were crossed and on one of his knees he was resting a brandy glass that was half full.

I could see little of his face, just a trace of grey beard here and there and the slight glint of light in two narrow eyes.

"Is that how Emily Chambers and Adam Hunter died?" I asked. "A simple injection into a part of the body where no one would look for marks – especially not you, a doctor. Is that how Mary was killed last night also?"

Dr Bernard took a drink from his glass and then placed it back on his knee. I noticed that his hand did not shake as he did so and that his drink did not slop one bit. He seemed eerily relaxed.

"There is no need for injections as ingestion of the poison works just as fast," he then said, calmly. "The tip of the needle is simply inserted between the sleeping victim's lips and the plunger used to administer a dose straight down the throat strong enough to kill ten men. The body is then rocked by violent seizures for a few seconds before falling still. The victim's heart stops beating within a minute. They are never even aware of what has happened."

"But that's not how Angela killed her father, is it?" I said, wondering where she was. I knew she would be in the house somewhere and so I kept my wits about me. "No, Jeffery Parsons died more violently, didn't he?"

Dr Bernard finished his drink and reached over to the small table next to him, the flickering of candle flames illuminating his face a little more as he poured another brandy from a decanter. I noticed that he was smiling. "Her father deserved it, and I thought it to be a very appropriate means of death after what he had done. You know it was his decision to abort the child, do you not? But do you know how it was done at such an early stage of pregnancy?" He drained his glass in one mouthful and then poured another immediately. "A mixture of medicines was forced down Angela's throat, Mr Attwood, to induce a miscarriage. Her father held her down whilst *my* father administered the chemicals."

I stared at Dr Bernard, assuming I had misheard him. "*Your* father?"

"Yes," he replied, "he was their family doctor. The man who was paid by Jeffery Parsons to go against his oath and become a killer of an unborn child. The man who, urged by Jeffery Parsons to save his own reputation, then certified Angela as insane and had her imprisoned in an asylum many miles from home where no one would believe what had been done to her. When I discovered where she was, I applied to work there, claiming I wished to study psychiatry whilst offering my services as a medical practitioner at the same time. Not that my career mattered. I really just wanted to be with Angela."

I tried to let this new revelation sink in. "And your father? The man you took over this practice from after he retired. Did she kill him, too?"

"She would have," Bernard said, as if it was nothing, "but a heart attack took him first, only a year into his retirement. That was four years ago, and our plans were not yet in place to go after those that had wronged her. We decided that we had to lie low after leaving the asylum and taking over the practice here in London. We had to bide our time."

There was something still bothering me about all of this.

"Why did you help her?" I asked. "Why did you decide to help someone you knew was so intent on revenge she would become a killer?"

"Why?" he asked, as if surprised that I did not understand. "I take it you have no children, Mr Attwood. If you did, then you would understand everything. If someone took away *your* child, *you* would do anything to get revenge."

And suddenly, I understood it all.

"You were the father," I said. "The letter Angela had been writing was meant for you."

"Yes." He took another drink and then swirled the liquid around the glass, staring at it, almost hypnotically. "She told me about that letter years later, as obviously I never received it. It was only because she never used my name that my identity was never discovered. Even when threatened with the forced abortion, Angela never told her father who had gotten her pregnant, knowing that it would mean no difference to the fate of the child but all the difference to mine."

"So, I take it the two of you met through your father being her family doctor?" I asked.

Bernard nodded. "During holidays from my medical studies I would assist my father in his practice. One time, we visited Mr Parsons to treat him for a painful flare up of gout. It was there that I met Angela. She was sixteen and I was eighteen. We fell in love almost instantly and wished to pursue a relationship. However, she told me that her father was a strict man who did not wish for her to marry so young. He wanted her to teach the word of the Lord and remain pure. I also knew my own father did not wish for the opposite sex to come in the way of my career. He would often remind me that when I was forty and a successful doctor, I would have my pick of young beauties so not to bother with them during my youth. We never told them about our feelings for each other and even tried to hold them back ourselves. But Angela and I were drawn to each other, like moths to a flame, and would meet illicitly whenever we could." His eyes suddenly narrowed more, his face twisting with suppressed anger. "When she found out she was pregnant, we knew we could not inform our fathers and so she arranged to go to an institution near Brighton, to a place for fallen women to have children out of wedlock and be cared for until their situation improved. Her father believed she was going to teach the Bible to the women there and so he agreed, pleased that his daughter was spreading the word of God to sinners. Anyway, we planned to meet up and marry in a year or so when I had finished my studies, but it was not meant to be." He drank more of his brandy and then smiled to himself. "I knew you would come here, Mr Attwood. I knew you were onto something. I suspected as much the first day you came here, asking strange questions. Then to see you turn up at Emily Chambers' funeral? I found it very strange, so I kept my eyes on you and noticed you head off and follow someone in the cemetery after the service. I waited in my carriage, not far from the church gates, and when you and the lady left, I had my driver follow you. I recognised the lady as the sister of William Hunter and when I saw you both go to St Simon's Hall, I knew you were on your way to discovering the truth." He chuckled, as if remembering something funny. "I actually thought you saw me that day, when the door blew open in the wind, but obviously you did not. Afterwards, when I followed you to the police station, I was certain that you were joining the dots to this little mystery. That is why Angela came to your house. She came for you, to put an end to your meddling, but found Miss Hunter in your bed instead and so decided to put an end to you both. When Angela told me that you had evaded her, I volunteered my services to the police the next morning. I knew by the way you were acting that you did not suspect me of anything but when I heard you mention Angela by name, I knew you would soon find out more."

"You're a clever man," I said, looking behind to the door, knowing Angela would come for me at some point. It was obviously the only reason Dr Bernard was telling me all of this was because I was not going to live to tell another soul. "You knew I'd go to the asylum. You assumed that I would find out about your time there and put two and two together."

"Finding out that I worked there would not prove anything," he said. "But finding out what Angela really looked like would prove everything. I knew there was at least one photograph that she was in, and Miss Granger also. I assumed because of your profession that you might notice it."

"Miss Grainger," I said. "Another one Angela killed?"

Dr Bernard nodded slowly. "She was my third assistant during the time I worked there. I hired her because of her physical resemblance to Angela and because she had no living relatives. Her death was nothing personal."

"You just needed people to think her body was Angela's," I said. "Yes, I guessed that much. Also, Angela could disguise herself as your assistant to make her escape."

Bernard nodded again. "On the night of the fire, I took Miss Grainger to Angela's room, just like I normally would when making my rounds and administering medication. She was poisoned – and that time it *was* by injection." He smiled, as if proud of his cunningness and I suddenly felt even more hatred towards this man. "Angela then dressed in Miss Grainger's uniform and cloak. With Miss Grainger's body in Angela's room, we then started the fire and left. When it was discovered soon afterwards, Angela, covering her face from the smoke, was evacuated along with the other female staff as we, the male members of staff, tried to tackle the fire. I was already due to take over my father's practice and so we simply left the next day for London."

"And plan your revenge?"

Dr Bernard nodded, slowly.

"Why go after their innocent children though?" I asked, thinking about Emily and Adam. "Why not just go after Chambers, Hunter and Burke?"

"We intended to do just that," he said. "Angela knew their names and I just had to search records to find addresses and hope that they all were still alive and living locally. To my surprise, one of them – Mr Chambers – was even one of my father's patients! Then I found that all of them were fathers themselves and our plan changed. We decided we would do to them what had been done to us. We would take their children, so that they would finally understand what we went through."

I checked behind me again. It was still all clear – for now.

"How did Angela get into the houses, though?" I asked. "She couldn't walk through walls or appear in a bedroom in a puff of smoke."

"We researched the houses," Bernard said, quite matter-of-factly. "Remember, this was five years in the planning. Once we found out where each family lived, we just had to watch them and learn their routines, find their weaknesses. We decided that the best time to act would be around the hour of three in the morning. Most people are in a deep slumber by then as the body is at its lowest ebb and therefore less likely to wake at the slightest noise. We wanted the death to seem natural, you see. We did not want to leave behind a sign of an intruder. The only thing we wanted to leave behind was a sign to let the father know that Angela had taken the life of their child."

"That's why she left a lily with the bodies, to remind the fathers of what they did," I said. "The lesson of the resurrection. To know that Angela had returned."

"Very good, Mr Attwood," he said. "The Hunter's household was not very secure and so that was relatively easy to enter. That is why we started with young Adam. Also, he was not a patient of mine and we wanted to see if his doctor would pick up on the signs of poisoning or simply put the death down to a seizure or a bad heart – which of course, he did. Anyway, having checked the house one night, we discovered that the living room window had no lock on the inside. Even better, on the outside, there was a small gap between the sill and the frame, enough to fit in several slim fingers and slide the window up fully. Once we tested it and made sure it could be opened and closed fully from the outside with little noise then we knew we had found our way inside. Angela was in and out of there within minutes without anyone seeing or hearing anything."

"And Emily Chambers' house?" I asked. "How did she get inside there?"

"That involved a little help from her father."

"What do you mean?"

"Like I told you, Mr Attwood, we watched the families for quite some time to learn their routines. Mr Chambers always went out on the first and third Saturday of the month to a gentleman's club to meet up with colleagues and discuss business. He would leave in his carriage at seven-thirty and return around ten-thirty. The others inside the house would retire to bed around nine, judging by when the lights went out. When Mr Chambers returned, he would unlock the door and leave it unlocked until his driver put the horses away for the night before following him inside about ten minutes later, locking the door for the night behind him. As my role as family doctor, I had been inside the house several times. I knew the layout. I knew there was a large cupboard under the stairs that contained only cleaning materials that no one would need during the night. Angela simply waited outside and made her way in after Mr Chambers and hid inside that cupboard until everyone was sound asleep."

"But then how did she get out?" I asked. "The front door was locked. She was trapped."

"You are forgetting that I am their family doctor," he said. "I knew I would be called the next morning. When Angela heard me arrive and head up the stairs to Emily's bedroom, she knew it would be safe to leave, which she did, quickly and quietly. She was already dressed in her work uniform and so if she had been seen she could have simply said that she had accompanied me as my assistant."

I could not believe what I was hearing. Instead of the deaths being the cause of some supernatural revenge, the actual killings had been planned, the prey stalked like animals. It all sounded very dirty and disgusting to me.

"And my house?" I asked. "How did she get in there?"

Bernard's smile widened. "Let us just say that your talkative cleaning lady thinks she has misplaced her keys. Like I have already told you, you roused my suspicions during our first meeting. I read your address on your mobile darkroom and had Angela go to your home the next morning to keep an eye on your actions. She saw your cleaning lady use a key to let herself in. Yesterday, when we decided that you had to be dealt with, we invited Miss Dawson here with an offer of work. As I showed her around, Angela took the keys from her bag. There were only four or five in there and so we assumed that one was for your house, which, of course, one was."

I shook my head in disgust. No wonder the door had been unlocked the next morning. I must have locked it before bed after all. It still did not make Mary's death any easier to stomach, though.

"And Inspector Burke's children?" I asked. "I take it you planned to kill them next? Tonight?"

"Indeed," Bernard said, calmly. "They were left until last as this would be the first time two deaths would occur in one night. Also, the family moved to a new house last year and so we had to research things a little more. Fortunately, the property next door to them has recently become vacant and we have managed to find a way inside – again through an unlocked window. After looking around we found that the loft space for the two houses is connected."

"So, Angela sneaks into the empty house and enters the loft," I said, guessing the plan. "She goes down through the hatch that leads down into Burke's house, kills the children and then escapes the same way she got in. All windows and doors remain locked inside Burke's house and so people think that no one could have gotten in at all."

"Well done, Mr Attwood." Bernard suddenly reached for the candle stand and stood up, the flickering light making his face look older, scarier, crazier, as he walked towards me, stopping an arms-length away.

"Pity you won't get away with it," I said, standing my ground. "Burke's not stupid. He'll find out how she got in."

"But only after he has learnt what it feels like to have someone else take away his children."

I gritted my teeth in frustration and stared Bernard in the eyes. I hated this man, and his evil partner Angela Parsons too. They had to be stopped.

"And I take it you're telling me this because I won't live to tell anyone else?" I asked, rhetorically.

Dr Bernard laughed and said, "It appears we are both clever men, Mr Attwood."

He did not know just how clever I was, obviously. Dr Bernard's face was illuminated by the candles he held, his eyes reflecting the light, so they acted like mirrors. I could see a faint reflection of myself in them. I could also see the black shape that was coming up behind me quickly and so I turned on my heels fast to defend myself.

Angela, dressed in her cape and hood, suddenly screamed as she ran at me, one hand raised above her head. Something she held glinted briefly and I saw that she had picked up the glass needle from the cabinet behind me. She was holding it like a dagger, her thumb on the plunger, ready to stab the poison into me.

I quickly dodged to the side and, working instinctively, I stretched out my leg. Angela could not react in time and her momentum sent her tumbling over my foot. As she did so I reached around, grabbed the back of her head, and pushed hard, sending her crashing into Bernard.

I heard the collision and the wind escape Bernard's mouth in a painful gasp. Then I was about to flee the room when I heard Angela scream "No!"

I stopped and looked back.

Bernard was staggering on unsteady feet, the needle jutting from the soft flesh at the base of his throat. He did not have time to pull the needle free before he collapsed to the floor and started to convulse violently, the candlestand spilling from his hand and rolling towards the window as he did so, the flames instantly licking away at the delicate lace curtains.

Angela sank to her knees beside him, wailing in despair. I could not help but stand and watch as Bernard's body twisted and writhed, his muscles clenching, his face contorting, before falling still a few seconds later. I noticed that his eyes had remained open throughout his final torment, focused squarely on the woman who had killed him. His beloved Angela.

"It's over," I said, feeling no pity for her. No matter what she had been through herself, she was a killer, a maniac. My sympathy lay with her victims and not with her.

When she was sure Bernard was dead, she turned and glared at me. The hood had fallen back from her head, and I could now see her face fully, including the bruise on her forehead she had received after our tussle outside my bedroom the previous night. She no longer looked like the prim and proper professional I had met two days earlier - she looked insane. Her eyes, brimming with tears, were locked on mine as she began to sob like a child.

"The police will be here soon," I told her as I became very much aware of the fire that was spreading by the window.

Angela looked back at Bernard, at the needle protruding from his throat and wailed like a banshee, a sound that sent shivers racing through my entire body. Then the wail turned into a scream as she turned back to me, her lips pulled back in a grimace born out of sheer rage.

She quickly jumped to her feet and raced forward, and I did not have a chance to react this time.

Angela dove into me with what seemed like the force of ten men, and I landed hard on my back, my head thudding against the wooden floorboards. Within a second, she was straddling me, screaming into my face as she closed her hands around my throat, digging her thumbs deep into my windpipe, squeezing the air from my lungs and stopping any more from entering.

Behind her, I saw flames rise as the entire curtains became engulfed and the room began to fill with choking black smoke.

Angela either did not seem to notice the danger or care about it as she tightened her grip around my neck. She was still screaming as she did so, staring down at me with madness and hatred, spit drooling from her bottom lip.

I tried to fight her off, landing blows to the side of her with my fists and smashing my knees against her back but they seemed to have no effect on her.

(Help me!)

I suddenly became aware of Emily's voice inside my head.

(Help me, pleeeease…)

But it was too late. My sight was beginning to fade, and my mind was starting to shut down. I was weak from my travels and lack of sleep and Angela Parsons was crazed. I could not stop her. Then, just as I thought I was about to die, I saw something appear through the smoke behind her, the black plumes parting like the Red Sea. It was Emily, standing there, looking down at us both with her painted eyes.

"Help me..."

I heard her voice clearly this time, even above the mad woman's screams and the roar of the flames and I watched as Emily quickly disappeared again within the smoke engulfing the room.

Then something happened that I did not expect.

Angela's eyes flickered with surprise. She stopped screaming and quickly looked behind her, as if she expected to see something other than Dr Bernard's body and the inferno that had spread along the wall and was now in danger of engulfing the entire room. Whether she had heard Emily's voice or not did not concern me right then. Survival was all I craved and so I took my opportunity and used all my reserves of strength to sit up and push Angela away from me.

My aim was better than I could have hoped for.

She fell back into the burning curtains, her weight and momentum ripping them away from the window where they settled upon her. Her scream became one of terror as she twisted and spun to free herself of the flaming material, but it was no use. The curtains had wrapped themselves around her like a flaming shroud and she could do nothing about it. Her fate had been sealed.

A moment later, Angela fell to the floor. Soon after that, her screaming stopped, she ceased thrashing, and fell still.

As the flames consumed her body, I passed out.

30
ESCAPING DEATH

"Wake up, Charles. You must wake up!"

The voice belongs to Emily. She is standing over me. No longer is she held up by my apparatus. No longer are her eyes closed. She looks alive and vibrant.

"It is over," she says. "Thank you."

I suddenly feel hands on my shoulders, pulling me away from her, away from the flames that have taken over the room, away from danger...

There was nothing but darkness for a long time, and no sound at all. Then, I suddenly felt a surge of energy, like someone had breathed fresh life into me, and my eyes snapped open.

"Em... Emily..." I croaked.

"You're alright, Charles," a deep, familiar voice said. "Just take your time and breathe."

I then became aware that I was suddenly very cold and wet. I sat up in the snow and coughed several times. My throat was dry and parched from the smoke I had inhaled. I was outside in the middle of the street. Across from me, Dr Bernard's house was still on fire, the flames now leaping out of a broken window, and Edward - good, brave, wonderful Edward - was standing over me.

"Lucky I got here when I did," he said.

"You saved me?" I croaked.

"Was nothin', Charles." He looked at the burning building and put his hands on his hips. "I take it things didn't go as you'd planned?"

I tried to stand and failed, falling back into the snow. Edward helped me the second time and kept one hand on my shoulder to steady me.

"Dr Bernard and Angela are dead," I said. "They'll never answer for their crimes and it'll never be proven that they were involved at all."

As soon as the words left my mouth, several horse-drawn vehicles rounded the bend in the road in the distance, the whistles of their occupants echoing around the street as they came towards us.

"It's the police," Edward said. "I told them to tell Inspector Burke that you were here, and *only* to tell inspector Burke, even if it meant waking him up at home. I thought it'd be the quickest way. After that I came back here to see if you needed help, and apparently you did." He looked at the police carriages coming closer, the horses that were pulling them struggling through the thick blanket of snow. "Come on, Charles, let's go before they get here."

"I should stay and explain," I protested, trying to shake my head into some form of clarity.

"I'll take you home and you can deal with this tomorrow," Edward said. "You're in no fit state to explain yourself now."

I was too weak to argue.

So, as the police vehicles came closer, Edward helped me into his carriage, and we escaped into the night as Dr Bernard's home continued to burn behind us.

31
MOVING FORWARD

I awoke to the sound of church bells ringing and sat up quickly.

To my initial surprise, I found that I was in my own bed and my first thoughts were of Mary and how she had been found dead here. I could still smell her sweet scent on the blanket and pillow and for the next several minutes I thought about our brief time together and cursed the fact that it had been tragically cut short. I then pushed my remorse aside and wondered how I had gotten back home. I soon remembered that Edward had rescued me from the fire, but I could not recall what had happened next. I did not know whether he had left me at my front door or helped me inside or even helped me to bed (I was still fully clothed, so he might have). Whatever he had done, I would be forever grateful to him.

I climbed out of bed, groaning at the stiffness in my back and neck and looking at the stains on my hands and clothes. I stank of stale smoke and my head throbbed not unlike my usual hangover as I walked to the window and threw open the curtains.

The morning was calm and bright, and the heavy snow had almost stopped, more than a foot having settled on the ground. Only a few delicate flakes still sauntered lazily to the earth.

I stood there a while, looking out onto this Christmas morning, listening to the church bells and watching the children play in the street below, throwing balls of snow at one another. They were laughing and shouting and having fun. Then I saw a man approach my house. He noticed me at the upstairs window and pointed to the door, as if asking if I would let him in.

It was Burke.

I knew he would come.

"Merry Christmas, Charlie," he said when I opened the door and felt the cold air nip at my nose and ears.

"Are you here to arrest me?" I asked, somewhat sarcastically.

Burke remained straight-faced. "Can I come in?"

I opened the door fully and stepped aside. Burke stamped his feet to rid them of the clinging snow and entered, heading into my study without waiting for an invitation.

"We need to talk, Charlie," he said taking a seat.

"I guess we do," I replied, sitting also. From outside, I could still hear the children playing. It soothed me slightly.

Burke inhaled deeply, as if to give him time to get his thoughts in order. Then, finally, he said, "I had a funny old night. Can you guess where I was?"

"Dr Bernard's office," I said, without hesitation. "You know I was there also, so let's stop messing about. You got a message to say I had gone there and when you arrived it was burning to the ground. So, like I said before, I assume you're here to arrest me?"

Burke shook his head. "We would've come for you before now if we were going to do that. Besides, this is my day off. The fire has been reported as accidental."

I did not quite understand. "I'm not a suspect?"

Burke winked. "You weren't even there, Charlie-boy."

"But Edward came to the station and reported that I was there and for you to come and get me."

"That doesn't matter," Burke said. "Paperwork goes missing all the time. There's no evidence to say that you were anywhere near that place last night or that anyone reported that you were."

I nodded, slightly relieved, but also feeling slightly unfulfilled. I knew Burke was covering for me, but I had to tell him what had happened and why it had happened.

"Dr Bernard and Angela Parsons were responsible for the murders," I said. "All of them, from Jeffery Parsons to Adam Hunter and Emily Chambers." I then explained about my trip to All-Hallows and what I had discovered there. Then what had happened at Bernard's office afterwards.

"I believe you, Charlie," he said. "I believed you not long after you ran away from me yesterday. I believed you so much that someone else was responsible that I've already submitted paperwork to acquit Arthur Olsen of the Jeffery Parsons murder."

"You're letting him go?" I asked.

Burke nodded and said, "Lack of evidence. Many homeless people could have used that old hall and committed the murder. We need to investigate more."

"And what will you find?" I asked.

Burke shrugged. "People will forget about Jeffery Parsons. In a few months no one will remember his murder and his case will be filed as unsolved."

I blew out my cheeks and sat back in the chair. Outside, I could still hear the bells ringing and the children playing. "So, what happens now? What do we do about all of this?"

"We can either tell the truth, or tell some lies," Burke said.

"We don't need to lie," I told him. "There's a photograph of Angela, Dr Bernard and the real Miss Grainger at the asylum. If we can find a photograph of Bernard and the fake Miss Grainger from within the last five years, then we can prove

Angela had escaped the fire and that Bernard was helping her."

Burke shook his head. "Dr Bernard's building was totally gutted by the fire, so if there were any photographs of Angela posing as his assistant then they no longer exist." He sat forward and gave my knee a friendly jab. "Do we really want to dig all of this up, Charlie? Do we want to try and prove all you say and maybe fail, and have you become a suspect in an arson that resulted in two deaths? Do we want to involve Mr and Mrs Chambers and tell them their daughter was murdered but that we can't prove it?"

I was unsure about what my friend was telling me. After all the corruption and lies I had discovered over these last few days, lying myself seemed such a hypocritical thing to do.

"But telling the truth is the right thing to do," I said. "Isn't it?"

Burke pulled out his hip flask and took a drink. He offered me some and I refused without even thinking about it.

"Maybe sometimes doing the right thing is not always the best thing," he then said. "If we tell the truth and can't prove your story then you're for it. You could be accused of starting the fire and killing two innocent people. The best thing is to pretend you were never there."

I sat quietly for a moment, trying to digest all of this. Then I asked, "What about Mary's death?"

"We know how she died," he said, "and who did it. There're dead, Charlie. I don't need a doctor to run any tests, so we put her death down to natural causes." He smiled, tight-lipped. "Justice has already been done for her, thanks to you. What else is there to do?"

I nodded, understanding where my friend was coming from. "What about Edward, though, Mr Chambers' driver? He knows all of this too. He took me to the asylum and rescued me from the fire."

Burke thought for a moment and then asked, "Do you think he'll say anything to Chambers?"

I honestly did not. Edward only seemed to speak when spoken to, and I doubted that Mr Chambers would ask him what had happened on our little trip. Even if he did, I strongly doubted if Edward would tell him the painful truth. So, I finally said, "No, Edward won't say anything."

Burke nodded.

"What do you say?" he asked. "Do we put all of this behind us?"

I sat there in silence for a while, going over all that had happened and all that I had learnt. In the end, my decision came down to a simple equation; would the truth make a difference for better or worse for those left behind.

"Yes," I then said. "It's best we say nothing."

"Good," Burke replied. Then he added, "One last thing."

"What's that?" I asked.

"Thanks for saving my children," he said, seriously.

I looked at the state of my clothes and felt the aches and pains that ran throughout my entire body.

"It was nothing," I replied.

I shook my friend's hand and saw him to the door. As he stepped outside, he asked me if I had anything planned for my Christmas day.

"Sleeping," I told him. My bed was all I needed to make this day special.

"If you get hungry you know where I live," he said.

"Actually, I don't," I replied, and could not help but laugh.

Burke finally told me his new address and said if I wanted to join them for dinner then I would be more than welcome. They were eating around one o'clock. I said I would think about it and stayed at the door as he headed off across the street where a young boy tossed a snowball at him, striking him on the shoulder. I laughed as Burke scooped up some snow and retaliated, the boy running away squealing with delight as Burke missed with his shot.

When my friend was out of sight, I stayed at the door a while longer, simply watching the children play.

32

SUMMING UP

So that is my story. Whether you believe it or not is up to you, but I have recounted it truthfully. I suppose I should also tell you some of the things that happened afterwards, so I will, briefly...

Mary was buried in the cemetery at St John's church beside her parents, not far from the graves of her brother, nephew, and sister-in-law. Her death was indeed recorded as natural causes and no one of authority asked any questions about it. I attended the service, as did Burke, Edward and, to my surprise, Mr Chambers. I still visit her grave regularly, as I do Emily's, both of their headstones now weathered and aged with time.

My friend, Andrew Burke, continued to work as a detective, retiring in 1887, only one year before the Jack the Ripper murders captured the national headlines. To this day, he is still happily married to Diana. His two children are married with children also. I attended both of their weddings.

Mr and Mrs Chambers remained a couple until the death of Mr Chambers in 1878. He died of a tumour in the stomach. I attended his funeral and have not seen his wife since. I believe she is still alive.

Edward also died not long after his employer, in the summer of 1880. We had remained close since we had been brought together through the events I have recounted, and his death affected me more than anyone since Mary's murder. Fortunately, Edward died a more natural death. A heart attack in his sleep.

Dr Bernard and the woman known as Miss Grainger were buried at St Mary's church, in the Bernard family plot. It had been stated in Bernard's will that the two of them should be buried in the same grave no matter how far apart their deaths. Some people thought it funny for a doctor to have his assistant spend eternity with him. I, however, did not.

As for myself, well, slowly but surely, life returned to normal after that Christmas. Miss Dawson arrived the following Monday and apologised for misplacing her keys and I told her not to worry and had another cut for her. I never touched alcohol again as I concentrated all my energy into my photography – my first exhibition being held a year later on the subject of hospitals and hospices which was quite a success. I included All-Hallows in the exhibition but with no mention of Angela Parsons. A few years later I eventually started teaching the craft of photography to others at a certain hall that had come up for sale along with an attached house at auction in the Spring of 1868. The first thing I did when renovating the place was to have the secret passage bricked up. The second thing I did was to have Jeffery Parson's house demolished. I taught at the hall until I retired at the age of sixty. The hall was demolished the year after I retired, the land purchased by the council for them to build more houses and extend the street and therefore affording me a comfortable living. I never married nor fathered any children, yet I was never lonely, so do not pity me.

As for Emily? I never saw her again. I take it I had done what she had wanted and had found peace. Either that, or *I* had found some sort of peace. I still think of her, as I do all the people in this story, although some of them with more fondness than others.

And that is it, I suppose.

Oh, apart from the dream. It still haunts me from time to time. Not every night, like it used to. Now it is more irregular, but it still comes, as if to remind me never to turn my back on anyone in need again.

As I finish writing this, it is a winter's night in 1901, the year Victoria died and was replaced on the throne by her son. Outside, the wind is blowing, and the snow is falling, and it is time for bed.

Maybe, quite possibly, the dream will come tonight to haunt me once more.

I hope so.

THE END

AUTHOR'S NOTE

Although the practice of post-mortem photography was indeed common during the Victorian era, I have taken certain liberties with the way it has been depicted in the preceding story. The consensus amongst historians and photographic experts is that there is no evidence to suggest that any apparatus was ever used to have the deceased held up in a standing position. Any photographs seeming to show such equipment were either used on living models (the poles and clamps were used to keep the person still during longer exposure times) or were deliberate hoaxes. However, being aware of the myth of such a technique led me to include it in *Memento Mori* as I felt it added a more unsettling quality to the story I wanted to tell. I hoped you enjoyed reading it. Thank you.

Lee Stevens